FAT VAMPIRE 3:
All You Can Eat
by Johnny B. Truant

Johnny B. Truant's
FAT VAMPIRE 3: All You Can Eat

A NOTE ABOUT THIS BOOK

I'm one of the three hosts of a podcast called *Better Off Undead* (which you can find at betteroffundeadshow.com and all the usual podcast places) and on episode 6 of that podcast, we asked the question, "If a vampire offered to turn you into one of his kind, would you accept?"

Dave, our resident "fat guy and proud of it," said that he'd take the deal.

My co-host Sean and I said that maybe that wouldn't be such a great idea for Dave, because if you're out of shape when you're turned, you might stay out of shape for all of eternity.

So I wrote a whole series of books about that single dumb idea, and what you're about to read is the third of them.

Enjoy.

For all the fat vampires out there.

FAT VAMPIRE 3: All You Can Eat
by Johnny B. Truant

STRIPPERS

REGINALD WAS GETTING TIRED OF bumping into strippers.

"Hey," he said to one of them the fourth time he ran into her next to the island in his kitchen, "you're going to have to stop getting between me and my refrigerator." And then he flashed his fangs at her.

"Are you a vampire?" said the girl.

"Yes."

"My manager is a vampire," she said.

The stripper's manager was across the room, wedged between the ottoman and the wall. His name was Vito and he had a giant feather in his hat. He was as much a vampire as Reginald was a swimsuit model. And Reginald, who would be three hundred and fifty pounds of bloodsucker until the end of his nearly-immortal life, was no swimsuit model.

Nikki raised her arm from across the room. "Hey, Raven Exotica," she said. "Come on over here, dear."

Raven Exotica, whose real name Reginald suspected might not actually be Raven Exotica, walked over to Nikki. Nikki guided the girl down to the floor, bent over her neck, and sank her fangs into her. Blood welled under Nikki's lips. A small red drop snaked its way into the hollow at the base of her neck.

"Don't kill her," said Reginald. "Just keep her out of my way. I had a tone there for a second, but don't go interpreting that as me desiring murder."

Reginald had learned a lot about being a vampire in the eleven months he'd been one, and one handy tip was that it was almost always a bad idea to drain humans until they were dead. You sucked out a bit more blood than the Red Cross would, you sealed the wound with a drop of your own blood, you glamoured them into forgetting you, and you sent them on their way. Doing it that way was much cleaner than murder, and usually invited no comeuppance from the authorities.

These days, the "sip and ship" method of feeding was the norm. There were still vampires who killed, of course, but most of them were sociopaths who would have snapped (or did snap) back when they were human. It was perfectly legal by vampire law to kill humans, but it was increasingly frowned upon. Once, Nikki had compared killing humans to smoking. It was still acceptable, but less and less in vogue as the years went on.

Sipping and shipping also sat well with Reginald's conscience. Less than a year ago, Reginald had been human. Just a few months ago, Nikki had been human. They'd been upstanding people back then, and the fact that they now needed human blood to survive hadn't changed the fact that neither enjoyed spilling it unnecessarily.

"I'm not going to *kill* her," said Nikki, rolling her eyes. Before being turned, Nikki was the kind of person who caught spiders in her house and released them outside rather than stepping on them.

Reginald walked over to where Nikki was slumped with Raven Exotica. "I know you wouldn't do it intentionally, but..." he began. He indicated the girl, who had collapsed into a limp rag as Nikki drank from her. "Just look at her color. She's as empty as a spent juice box." He pointed to the brunette in hot pants who had fallen under the dining room table. "That one is the fullest if you're still hungry. But the real question is, how the hell *can* you still be hungry?"

"I'm just *ravenous*," said Nikki. She pulled her fangs out of Raven Exotica, licked them clean, then reluctantly drew a drop of blood from her finger to heal the wounds on the girl's neck. "Food and sex. Sex and food. It's all I can think about. Maurice said this would pass."

But it *hadn't* passed, despite what Maurice had said. Nikki was young as a vampire, but she was well past infancy — a time that often engendered extreme thirst, both literal and sexual — and hence should have found it easier to be sated. But that hadn't happened. She still fed constantly, often going on three- or four-human binges, draining them well below Reginald's comfort level despite her compassionate nature.

Reginald thought he might have an idea what the problem was. He suspected that her thirst might be mental rather than physical. It was a topic that Reginald, who was currently heating taquitos despite the fact that he knew they'd pass through his vampire system almost unaltered, knew a thing or two about.

Reginald sometimes wondered if his weakness and slowness (he was only as strong and fast as a moderately fit human) had anything to do with the way he ate. He only took in enough blood to keep him alive, and constantly ate human food that tasted good but did nothing for him. Several times, to answer this question, he'd gone on a vampire diet. He wanted to ingest only healthy blood for two weeks to see if it made a difference, but he never made it through both weeks. He always ended up ordering Chinese food before the third day drew to a close.

For what it was worth, Maurice told him that changing his diet wouldn't make a difference. Reginald was stuck with the body he'd had as a human, and the only thing that would make him stronger or faster was time. A *lot* of time. Maurice couldn't say how much time was "a lot," but Maurice's perception was warped anyway. He'd been alive for more than two thousand years and thought of decades like most people thought of weeks.

Nikki crawled over to the girl under the dining room table. "*Chaaaaaastity*," she cooed. The girl looked over, then passed out. Reginald was going to need to watch her. Nikki was stronger than she knew, faster than she knew, and thirstier than her level of restraint seemed to realize.

Nikki did all of the hunting in the house. Because she was in a relationship with Reginald, she could only feed on women unless she wanted to appear unfaithful, so she did — often in groups. But whenever Reginald would allow it, Nikki would bring home a man for him. Reginald always acted as if he were a child being given medicine when it was time for him to feed. He said that blood was warm and gross. And what's more, he said he didn't like putting his lips on men's necks.

"I know it's crazy, but it's true." He told her. "In fact, if you can believe it, I almost *never* put my mouth on a man's neck when I was human."

Nikki, who'd always been a health nut, was undeterred. Rather than trying to force vampire habits on Reginald, she tried to work around them.

Once, for Reginald's birthday, she took a nursing class to learn how to start a needle in a donor's arm to collect blood. She bought the necessary supplies and then brought a man home, glamoured him, sat him in a chair, and began to collect his blood into Reginald's favorite coffee mug. It hadn't gone well. Nikki was terrible at glamouring, and her spell broke just after she'd started the needle but before she'd attached tubing to it. The terrified man had run around Reginald's living room, spraying the walls, floor, and couch with gore before Nikki drove him into a corner and knocked him unconscious with a chair.

When Reginald came home, Nikki, her hair askew and her clothing torn, had presented Reginald with a chilled cup and a smile. She'd stirred cocoa and Stevia into the donor's blood and had added a stick of cinnamon as a stirrer. She'd even topped the cup with whipped cream. But Reginald, who'd just returned from a particularly frustrating errand, saw only his blood-covered living room and began complaining that his favorite coffee cup had now been befouled with blood. Nikki threw the cup through Reginald's television and stalked out, shouting behind her that Reginald could do his own goddamn hunting from here on out.

Reginald later apologized, but Nikki hadn't tried to play nurse again. Instead, she occasionally brought home two or three women and one or zero men, and it was up to Reginald to do his part to get his dinner. She didn't care if he didn't want to eat, she told him. If that's how he wanted to be, he could just starve.

The final stripper returned from the bathroom, where Reginald later learned she'd gone in order to bleed all over his towels. Her name was Precious and she was just as drained as Raven Exotica. Reginald realized that he'd have to get them out of here very soon. He'd have to take them away before Nikki's hunger overcame her moral imperative to not accidentally kill people.

Then something dawned on him.

"Nikki, how did you get these people here?" he asked

"I writhed around one of the poles at the strip joint and told them I wanted to party. Who could resist this?" She ran a hand down her front, giggling as the hand reached her breasts.

"You didn't glamour them?"

"You remember what happened with the guy with the needle in his arm. I've pretty much given up glamouring. I rely on my *innate* glamour."

Reginald put his hands on his hips. "Well, guess what?" he said. "I didn't glamour them either."

Nikki looked at the four humans, her mouth opening. Across the room, Vito, the strippers' manager, succumbed to the ottoman and fell against the wall, where his face left a red smear.

"Wait..." she began.

"That's right. You're not looking at glamour-stupid people here. You're looking at serious, garden-variety anemia," said Reginald.

The stripper under the table tried to stand, rapped her head on the table's underside, and collapsed. On the floor behind the ottoman, Vito said, "Did I leave the iron on?"

"Oh," said Nikki.

"Not good, my darling," said Reginald.

"Oh."

"If they'd gotten away..."

"I know, I know."

But it was hard to be mad at her, because she was so clearly just being what she was: A vampire's vampire, from head to toe. It was ironic that they'd been a part of that whole episode a few months back — wherein vampires were accused of "losing the game against humans" — because Nikki, with her compulsive blood lust, was poised to win that particular game all by herself. Too bad doing so would put her on the wrong side.

Reginald rounded up the humans, sat them up against the wall, and met their eyes one by one. He told them an acceptable story about what had happened to them tonight, changed them into Salvation Army clothes that were in the storage closet for just such blood-soaked nights, and gave each a cookie.

"Like blood donors," said Nikki, watching the humans gum the cookies.

"Better than nothing."

"I'm sorry," she said.

"It's okay. I doubt they were ever any danger to us. Glamouring them was like glamouring a sponge. It was like using a sledgehammer to tune a piano."

"I don't understand that metaphor," said Nikki.

"I know."

"Maybe I should go see a vampire doctor about my problem."

"Nah, it's cool," said Reginald. "A lot of healthy people don't understand my metaphors."

They stared at the humans.

"We have to get them out of here. But if we carry them through the streets..." Reginald began.

"Garage," said Nikki.

Nikki carried the humans in a giant tottering pile by herself, seemingly as penance. It was like carrying too much laundry. Raven Exotica kept falling off the top of the pile, and Nikki kept stooping to grab her and toss her back up.

Once in the garage, Nikki arranged the four people in Reginald's car like she was playing dolls. Reginald noticed that she'd placed Precious's hand on Vito's crotch and decided that it was probably subconscious. Recently, in the grips of her neverending vampire hunger and horniness, she'd been buying porn without realizing she was doing it. She kept handing *Hustler* magazines to Reginald and saying, "I got you the new copy of *Wired*."

"I'll take them," she said. "I'll drop them off at the bowling alley."

"Nice. Lots of strippers hanging out behind the bowling alley?"

She gestured vaguely at the car. "Three of them anyway, plus their pimp."

"Manager."

"Sure. Manager."

She climbed into the car, opened the garage door to the dark night, and rolled down the window.

"Want me to come with you?" said Reginald, leaning down.

"Actually, no. I need the time. What happened tonight... it bothers me."

"Why?"

"It makes me wonder if I'm any different from the rest of them. From the assholes who tried to execute you."

Reginald shrugged. "You're a vampire. You were training and preparing to be a vampire for years before you became one. You knew the deal. This is who you are now. Maybe it's who you always were."

She looked away. "Don't say that."

He reached through the window and put his hand on her arm. "Nikki. You're still a good person."

She shook her head and shifted the car into reverse. "That's exactly the problem, Reginald," she said. "I'm not a person at all anymore."

BAD NEWS

NIKKI RETURNED IN BETTER SPIRITS. Reginald took it as a temporary reprieve.

Ever since being turned, Nikki had been subject to mood swings. Reginald wasn't sure what his role was supposed to be in helping her through her rough patches, or even if he had a role at all. She'd been turned right before the now-infamous "Ring of Fire" incident, and he'd feared even then that she was making an ill-informed, emotionally rushed decision. They'd had a few weeks of whirlwind activity followed by the almost-end-of-the-vampire-world, and after that, as things returned to their current state of abnormal normal, cracks in her armor had started to appear.

It was hard to blame her for being up and down. These days were enough to give even the most stalwart vampire pause. So Reginald decided to do the American thing and ignore it, hoping that the problem would go away on its own.

"They're happy," she reported, referring to the four anemic people she'd schlepped to the bowling alley. "I bought them Chunkies."

"Like, fat people?" said Reginald.

"Candy bars. *Chunky*. I thought you were a connoisseur." Then she looked from Reginald to the other side of the room, where Reginald had forgotten the TV was on. He didn't want her to see the news program he'd been watching, so he quickly clicked to another channel.

Nikki gave him a sarcastic smile that said, *You've got to be kidding me.* "Turn it back," she said.

"Nikki..."

"I'm not as fragile as you think I am. I'm a big girl. Now turn it back to the news or I'm going to screw you until you die, even if you can't die."

"Um...?"

"That was supposed to be an ominous threat. I forget why." Then she looked at a plate that was sitting on the end table. Reginald's taquitos had finished cooking while she was taking out the trash, and he was eating them with guacamole and sour cream.

"Taquitos," she said.

"Shut up, mom," said Reginald.

"It can't be healthy, the way you eat."

"I'm a vampire. Is this food going to kill me again?"

"Exactly. You're a vampire."

"I ate a whole dude earlier!"

She shook her head, as if he were a lost cause.

"I also just ordered a pizza from that all-night place," he added. "It will arrive shortly."

"How the hell can you still be hungry?"

"Really?" he said. "Three hookers *you* ate. *Three.*"

"Strippers."

"Give them a year," he said.

Reginald was in the middle of the couch. He had to reach all the way across the rightmost cushion to reach his plate of taquitos, which he did as Nikki stared at him. He supposed he should have moved the plate to the coffee table, but that seemed like entirely too much work.

Nikki picked up a throw pillow that was occupying the non-taquito side of the couch and tossed it onto a recliner. "Move over, fatass," she said, pushing him aside with her rear. Then she plopped down next to him, very close. Reginald was normally possessive about his personal space, but that didn't apply to Nikki. She leaned over and wrapped an arm around him.

"I'm serious about the TV," she said. "Please stop protecting me."

"It's just more of the same. Humans misinterpreting things, vampires being murdering fuckers. Neither of us need to hear about it. That includes me."

"Flip it back."

With a sigh, Reginald raised the remote and flipped back to the news.

On the screen, a newswoman with an immobile blonde hairdo was saying, "... south wing, and spread across the rest of the building quickly. Authorities are blaming a gas leak combined with improper ventilation for the spread of the fire..."

"Gas leak again," said Reginald. "Same as the time the roof blew off of the Council building. Why do humans blame everything they can't explain on gas leaks?"

"Shhh," said Nikki.

"... almost fifty fatalities. Henry Jacobs is live on the scene. What's the mood like there, Henry?"

The screen changed. The woman with the immobile hairdo was replaced by a man with an immobile hairdo.

"Wendy, the only word for it is 'devastated.' This neighborhood has been shaken by a tragedy of tremendous magnitude. Forty-seven people died last night when what used to be the Tremont Hills apartment building, behind me, caught on fire. Those who escaped are dumbfounded. Eyewitnesses say that the fire didn't seem to spread rapidly from the outside, suggesting that many of the deaths were due to smoke, blocked exits, or simply failing to get out in time. Those outside waited and waited for more people to emerge, but they never did."

"They'll get wise to it," said Reginald. "In fact, I'd bet the authorities that matter already are. You can tell whether people died in a fire or whether they were killed beforehand. They just must not want to alarm the public."

"Wise to what, though?" said Nikki. "They don't know what they're looking at. They might get that the fire was started to cover up something else. But drained, bitten people? What will that mean to them?"

"Hmm."

"We should do something," she said.

"Do what, exactly?" said Reginald. "There's nothing illegal going on here. Not by vampire law, anyway."

Nikki shook her head. "Murderers. We've become murderers."

"If by 'we' you mean 'vampires,' then 'we' have always been murderers. You joined this club willingly, my dear."

"To sip and ship. No respectable, sensible vampire kills people outright anymore. It's too hard to get away with, and it's just plain *wrong*."

Reginald nodded. Eleven months ago, he'd been a human. *Every* vampire had once been a human. But it changed nothing. How quickly some vampires forgot their human roots, and raised themselves above those they hunted.

"It's not as hard to get away with as you'd think, apparently," said Reginald, gesturing at the TV. "If you kill fast enough, they can't keep up. Or if enough parties are doing the killing, they can't pin any one of them down."

And that was the bigger problem. One killer could be caught. A race of killers was much harder to put a finger on. Since the Ring of Fire, the Vampire Nation as a whole had been absolutely terrified. Vampires seemed to feel that they had dodged a bullet, and that the end of their kind was looming if they failed to do what the angels wanted. The problem was that nobody *knew* what the angels wanted. Balestro and his kind had been mute since that night on the German hilltop. So the Nation panicked and the Nation fretted, and eventually the Nation begged to be told what to do in order to quell their terror — and vampires like Charles Barkley were all too eager to provide that direction.

Charles, prominent on the Council since Maurice deposed Logan, had stepped up with a three-stage plan designed to "right the game" that vampires were playing against humans, thus saving the species. Stage one was to kill and turn humans. Stage two was to kill and turn humans. Stage three was to kill humans, and maybe turn them.

"I can't watch this," said Nikki.

"I told you."

"And what kills me is that I'm part of the problem."

"No you're not. You're different."

"I've spilled my share of blood."

"Sip and ship," said Reginald. "It's no different for them than donating blood. They're just donating it to us."

She shook her head. "I was always conflicted as a human, Reginald. I loved animals, but I ate meat. How could I justify that? I couldn't. But I just let it go. I ate meat and I loved animals and I pretended that there wasn't a conflict. And now

I'm a vampire who is aghast at all of this murder, and yet I drink their blood."

Reginald shrugged. There was nothing he could say. She was determined to beat herself up. He couldn't change her mind, so his only option was to distract her.

He turned off the TV, then pointed into the corner. "Hey, look over there!"

She looked, then looked back at Reginald.

"What?"

"Nothing. But you were distracted for like a second, so it was worth it."

She raised her hand, about to grab something heavy and throw it at him, but at that exact moment, Reginald's doorbell rang. Nikki's eyebrows went up.

"My pizza," Reginald explained.

Reginald got up and tried to use his vampire super-speed to run to the door faster than Nikki could see, but instead he tripped over the ottoman, which was still soaked with Vito's blood and dusted with pieces of his shredded hat feather.

The doorbell rang again.

"Did you see my awesome speed?" said Reginald from the floor.

There was a blur above him. Nikki opened the door, then dragged the pizza man down beside Reginald, her hands pinning him to the carpet, her mouth on his neck.

Reginald, climbing to his feet, yelled down at Nikki. An answering yell came from the pizza man, but the pizza man's yell was much higher-pitched than he would have expected.

Reginald looked down. Around a mouthful of flesh, Nikki said, "It was a girl."

The pizza man, who'd turned out to be the pizza girl, was staring up at Reginald with terror. She'd stopped screaming, which was a good thing because the door was open. Reginald kicked the door closed, then kneeled over the pizza girl, over Nikki's back and greedily drinking head.

He looked into the girl's eyes and said, "You're into this. You've always been bi-curious."

Instantly, the terror left the pizza girl's face. Her eyes closed and she gave an erotic sigh.

"Oh, gross," said Nikki. She pulled away and looked at Reginald, her mouth covered with blood. "Make her less turned on."

"Why should I?" Reginald snapped. "You just cost me a pizza."

The twin punctures in the girl's neck were bleeding crimson blood into a pool on the carpet. The girl herself was oblivious to the wound. She was writhing and moaning in ecstasy, her hair soaked with carpet blood, changing from a dirty blonde to a wet red.

"No I didn't," said Nikki. She pointed to the coffee table, where a large pizza box was sitting among Reginald's magazines. She must have run the pizza to the coffee table before taking the girl down. Reginald hadn't seen it happen. Damn, she was fast.

Nikki returned her mouth to the girl's neck. The pizza girl began rubbing herself.

"*Grooooooss,*" Nikki moaned. "Reginald, snap her out of it!"

"Snap her out of it? Hell, I'm going to get the video camera."

Ten minutes later, Nikki stopped drinking and patched the girl's wounds. Then she changed the pizza girl's clothes and took her into the bathroom to wash her off — and then, seemingly because she felt guilty, she washed and braided the girl's hair. She did the last while wearing only a bra, having discarding her own bloody shirt. Reginald watched and made more video camera jokes.

When she was done and dressed, Nikki went to one of the blackout shades on Reginald's windows. She took a quick glance at the wall clock, then peeled back the shade to peer outside.

"I can't drive her home," she said. "It's too close to sunrise. If our overlords want us to evolve, when are they going to create those light-tight cars for us, like in that Ethan Hawke movie?"

Reginald assessed the girl and declared her fine to drive. He gave her a cookie, a big tip, and sent her on her way. As she was leaving, the girl asked Nikki to call her so that they could "go out for drinks sometime or something."

After she was gone, Nikki stood with her back to the door, her face troubled.

"I'm sorry. I don't know what came over me. I just couldn't help it."

"That's four," said Reginald. "*Four* humans in one night. I barely go through that many in a month."

"I was ravenous." Then a frightened look crossed her face. "And what's more, I've realized that I kind of... I kind of... Oh, it's *terrible*."

"What?"

"I guess I feel like I... I *want to hurt them*." She sat down and put her face in her palms.

"It might be blood ties," said Reginald, sitting beside her and putting a hand on her shoulder. "I've read a bit about it. It's like being psychically linked to those whose blood you share, and whose blood *they* share. Sometimes I hear Maurice in my head as if he's standing right beside me, and a time or two I've heard someone that I assume is Maurice's maker. I don't even know who he is, except that he has an accent. I sometimes get emotions directly from both of them, rather than from myself. It's unsettling."

"So?"

"So what I'm saying is, maybe it's not you. Maybe you're feeling anti-human sentiment that's coming from others, through your blood."

"But *you're* my maker! And *Maurice* is yours! Neither of you feel that way about humans."

Reginald shrugged. "Maybe you're reaching back farther. Maybe you're... particularly *good* at blood memory, or something."

"It's like I'm not in control. I feel like werewolves must feel. Part of me wants you to chain me up, for my own good."

"Hot."

"I'm serious," she said.

"I'm going to Maurice's tomorrow night" said Reginald. "Come with me. Maybe he has thoughts."

"Are you going there for Council business?" she asked.

Nikki missed Maurice and kept asking Reginald what, if anything, he was up to. He hadn't been at the office for more than two weeks, so she'd seen very little of him. Of course, Maurice didn't *need* to work because thousands of years plus some basic investments had made him very rich, but he seemed to enjoy the monotony of playing human, and it was time that they all had to be together.

"There are some Council matters we need to discuss, yes. It almost sounds like good news from the Nation if you don't look closely enough. For instance: Did you know that restrictions on wanton creation have been removed?"

"*Wonton* creation?"

"Don't I wish. No: *wanton*. It's what they tried me for, but now nobody is trying or punishing anyone for making new vampires without getting approval first."

"That's good."

"It looks that way, but this it isn't an equality move. It's an accelerant, to create more vampires quickly. Somehow, all of the fat, old, and disabled new recruits are meeting with suspicious accidents."

Nikki sighed. There was so much to be revolted by that she didn't know where to start.

"Chin up," said Reginald. "At least you got felt up by a pizza girl tonight."

PIMPING AND SUBTERFUGE

REGINALD KNEW NOTHING ABOUT WHERE Maurice lived except that it was close to the office, so he'd formed a mental picture based on the kinds of places that were nearby: Maurice would live in an aging, smallish two-story colonial with chronically peeling paint at its corners, like the house that Reginald lived in.

But he was wrong. Maurice didn't live close to the office at all. Reginald had decided that he did before he knew Maurice was a vampire, and hence before he realized that "Maurice comes to work on foot" didn't equate to "Maurice lives nearby."

It took Reginald and Nikki nearly a half hour to reach their destination the following night, and what they found when they arrived wasn't an aging colonial with peeling paint. The houses in Maurice's neighborhood were huge — and even amongst the houses in Maurice's neighborhood, Maurice's house was massive. It was a giant white palace with sprawling grounds pocked by Grecian statues that Reginald felt were probably authentic and definitely excessive. (Nikki wondered aloud if Maurice even knew that all of the statues were even there, considering that he never saw them during the daytime.) There were complicated hedges. There were tiered planters. The house itself was all pillars and parapets.

"He's rich," said Nikki.

"Yet he works with us," said Reginald.

"He's two thousand years old. I'll bet you run out of things to do when you're that old. He must work because he's bored. How much wealth can you create simply by existing longer than everyone else? How many fancy hedges can you plant and trim? How many novels can you write? How many paintings can you paint?"

"So what you're telling me," Reginald said, "is that given enough time to live and create and grow, we all default to selling treadmills in the end."

But Nikki didn't hear him. She'd walked up to a massive, grooved pillar and was stroking it, running her fingers along the stone. She jumped a little when Maurice appeared behind them, holding a sword in his hand. It took Reginald a moment to realize that it was the sword he carried all the time, including at the office.

"Hey," he said. "Sorry. I was trimming the hedges." He sheathed the sword, then walked between them and pulled the front door open, gesturing them inside. "Welcome to my humble abode."

The foyer was classic marble, but Maurice seemed to have added his own touches to make the rest of the decor less classic. There were beautiful iron sconces along the walls, but each had been draped with a blood red cloth, which gave the room a foreboding feel. There was a small fountain in the middle of the foyer (Reginald couldn't resist tossing a penny into it), but someone had done something to the water in it to turn it as black and opaque as ink. There were paintings on the walls in elaborate frames, but they were all black velvet and, Reginald thought, fairly tasteless. Gold was everywhere — accenting upholstered chairs that seemed to have no function, on lamps and scattered knickknacks, and gilding a massive mirror that was easily one and a half Reginalds tall.

Reginald walked over to the mirror and stood in front of it. The legend about vampires not casting reflections wasn't true — something Reginald gave thanks for every time he combed his hair, and something Nikki had given thanks for on the day she'd won an argument involving putting a mirror on the ceiling in the bedroom. Nikki thought the ceiling mirror was hot. Reginald thought it was traumatizing. He kept waking up and scaring himself into palpitations that, because he was a vampire, were merely painful and inconvenient.

In Maurice's massive mirror, Reginald didn't have a reflection.

"I can't see myself," he said.

"It's ancient glass," said Maurice, walking up to stand next to Reginald and gesturing at the still-empty reflection. "Back in the day, vampires really *couldn't* be seen in mirrors, just like the legends say. Our modern mirrors have changed that, designed in conjunction with vampire scientists in order to..."

A woman appeared deep in the mirror, smiled, waved, and started walking toward them. She said, "Maurice, you didn't tell me our guests were here!"

Maurice sighed dramatically and hung his head.

The woman became a blur and immediately appeared in front of Reginald, setting her hand affectionately on Maurice's arm. She was short, round, and unremarkable-looking. She was wearing a 1950s style dress and red heels, her reddish hair piled on top of her head.

She looked at Maurice's face and said, "What?"

"I was doing my mirror bit. And he was totally buying it."

Reginald walked forward and placed his hand on the mirror. Except that there was nothing there. He looked forward, then back over his shoulder. The views in each direction were identical, right down to the paintings on the walls and the trivial items placed on tables and other furniture. He looked at Maurice.

"You get bored," said Maurice. "One day in the 1700s, I said, 'What would it be like to have a corridor that was a mirror image of itself?' That's the problem with being immortal. Humans dismiss stupid thoughts like that, but I had nothing but time and money and was currently between jobs, so I had a new wing built and spent fifty years creating the little joke that my wife has just ruined."

"I'm sorry, dear," said Maurice's wife.

"And you're the first guests we've had in forever. Most of the time, I have to face the possibility that the fifty years I spent making my house into a mirror reflection of itself might have been a waste of time."

"I'm Celeste," said the woman, extending her hand, "since Maurice is too obsessed with his dumb optical illusion to introduce us."

Reginald shook Celeste's hand and introduced himself, then introduced Nikki. Nikki was still looking around the room with her mouth open. Nikki asked Celeste if she could have a tour. Maurice started to say something, but Celeste interrupted him and said that she'd be happy to.

It took almost an hour to tour the house, and Reginald still felt like they were rushing. The marble palace had three stories, and there was no coherent theme between stories or rooms, or even between different corners of any given room. Everything was ostentatious and looked like it cost a fortune, but most of it still somehow managed to be over the top and tacky. Reginald noted Warhol paintings next to Renaissance masterpieces (in a haphazard stack, leaning against a wall) next to ancient hulks that looked like they may have been the creations of inventors trying to build the first flying machines. Parts of the house looked like a

Trump hotel, parts looked like a rap star's blinged-out pimp palace, and parts looked like a museum.

"It's not hard to create a lot of wealth when you've had as much time as I've had," Maurice explained. "Back in the day, we didn't have mortgages and cars and flat-screen TVs, so those of us who didn't have to pay for food or medical care or any of the usual things just kind of socked away whatever money we had. Do you have any idea what an 1800 dollar is worth today? I had a lot of them, and they just kept piling up because I was bored, and therefore got jobs to pass the time. Then, when companies started selling stock, I bought a lot of it because I had no better way to spend what I had. Who knew Coca Cola would take off? And Ford, and GE, and Apple, and Microsoft?"

Maurice said that he would have been content to live somewhere dark and simple like a crypt, but that Celeste, who was half his age (and who Maurice saved from death by turning her, as he'd done with Reginald) had changed all of that. She wanted a roof. She wanted a garden, which she'd tend under the moonlight.

"I buy nice things," she said. "Maurice tries to do the same, but he has such terrible taste. Witness Exhibits A through D." She indicated three black velvet Elvis paintings and a life-size set of KISS costumes. "Upstairs, there's an army of stormtroopers and one of the original Darth Vader outfits. He's arranged them in a diorama, like life-size dolls."

Reginald started toward the stairs, but Nikki held his arm.

Celeste put her hand on Maurice's shoulder and rubbed it, smiling. They made an odd couple. Even though Maurice was much older, he looked much younger. If they were human, Reginald would have guessed Celeste would be in her late thirties, whereas Maurice was permanently nineteen. He was dark and goth, sporting black clothes, black fingernail polish, and a black shock of hair that was always over his face. She looked like a red-haired Donna Reed. Nikki and Reginald towered over both of them. It was like being hosted by dwarves — rich dwarves, with Mike Tyson's style sense.

Celeste gave Maurice's shoulder a squeeze and excused herself, explaining that she had a cake in the oven she needed to attend to.

When she was gone, Reginald said, "Cake?"

"She just makes them and throws them away," Maurice explained. "Neither of us has any taste for human food, but she likes to cook and bake. For a while, we tried to give her food away, but who donates fois gras to a homeless shelter? Rack of lamb? Pheasant under glass? Canapes and cannoli and souflees? The homeless people got really excited the first few times when we showed up, but then the organizers started to get curious. Who was this couple who had nothing better to do but to prepare extravagant food and never eat it? So we stopped. One thing I've learned is that it's never a good idea to invite curiosity if you're a vampire. It's always better to fade into the background."

Reginald was thinking that he could find a home for all of that food.

"I know what you're thinking, Reginald, but you don't need more encouragement. Your system will tolerate human food less and less as time goes on."

"Maybe I can keep my system used to it," said Reginald. "Like staying in shape by running every day."

"You could try that theory with... say... running every day," said Maurice.

"I have been," said Reginald. "Watch this." He ran as fast as he could to the end of the long faux-mirror corridor, then turned and sprinted back. When he was finished, his head was spinning. He bent forward at the waist and put his hands on his knees, panting.

"Impressive," said Maurice. "You might now be able to outrun a small human child. Like, under two, while their legs are still short."

Nikki rubbed Reginald's back. Reginald could feel his shirt sticking to him and cringed at how gross it must feel against Nikki's palm.

"I need to sit down," he said. "Someone get me cake."

Maurice shrugged and began walking down the mirror hallway in the direction Celeste had gone. He was strolling casually, allowing Reginald to decide whether to follow him or not. With great effort, Reginald did. Nikki held his hand to steady him. At first Reginald found it cute, since she was well under half his weight. But then he remembered that she was no longer a fragile human, and was many times stronger than he was.

When they got to Maurice and Celeste's dining room, Maurice sat at one end of a polished wood table and Reginald sat at the other. Nikki and Celeste sat on the sides. Everyone had a cup of warm blood ("We have a group of donors playing foosball in the basement," Celeste explained), and they sat and sipped as they talked.

Celeste, Nikki, and Reginald were drinking from gold cups that Reginald suspected might actually be gilded with real gold. Maurice's cup was an enormous bejeweled chalice with MAURICE spelled out in diamonds on one side and MOTHERFUCKER spelled out on the other side. When Nikki asked him about it, Maurice explained that the chalice had belonged to a famous rap star who'd gone bankrupt. Maurice had had the word RHYMING changed to MAURICE by a jeweler, but then one of the rap star's rivals had killed the jeweler and Maurice had never gotten around to having the cup finished.

Reginald had barely touched his blood. In front of him was a pot pie and a cheesecake. On his left, Celeste was beaming like a cliche Italian mother who's gotten someone to eat because they're too skinny.

"So," said Maurice.

Reginald didn't reply. He was trying to eat the pot pie, but he was so excited about Celeste's food that his fangs wouldn't retract. He kept biting the fork by accident, occasionally getting his fangs stuck between its tines.

"So," Maurice repeated.

"So that's some pimp cup you have," said Nikki, to break the awkwardness.

Maurice threw his napkin at Reginald.

"Yeah?" said Reginald. He sounded like he'd just been awoken from a nap.

"Charles," said Maurice.

"Reginald," Reginald replied.

"If you don't stop making love to that pot pie for long enough to talk to me, I'm going to take it away."

Reginald wrapped an arm around the plate. Then he set his fork down, wiped his mouth with Maurice's napkin, and looked up.

"Fine," he said. "Down to business, then. Here's my analysis as your resident fat mentat: Your days as an effective leader are essentially over. Charles has won."

Since the Balestro incident, Charles had gained significant power on the Vampire Council. It wasn't because he was a good leader or brilliant orator, but because he told the assembly what it wanted to hear. He'd also gone onto the protected vampire internet and begun spreading videos and written propaganda telling the populace what *it* wanted to hear. The Vampire Nation wasn't a democracy, but the will of the masses soon began to feel palpable. Everywhere Reginald and Maurice went, they could sense the eyes of other vampires on them, seeming to ask why the Deacon couldn't propose solutions as Mr. Barkley was doing... and if the Deacon was, therefore, fit to lead the Nation at all.

"He's won?"

"Hearts and minds. All he needs to do is to spout anarchist propaganda and tell vampires that they have power over humans that the angels want them to use. Even if he does that and nothing else, his position is already much, much better than yours. Think about it. What are *you* telling them? To legislate? To negotiate? Maybe to do some scientific research? *Booo-ring.*"

"I don't know what else to do," said Maurice. "There's no easy button to solve this problem."

"Sure there is," said Reginald. "It's just the wrong thing to do. A slow, methodical plan for change requires patience and small steps. Killing and turning thousands of people into vampires is easy. Every one of us knows how to do it. It's in our blood. And what's more, Charles can claim that he's trying to meet us halfway. You were against penalties for wanton creation, and he's removed them. You wanted to open up creative freedom, and now the Nation has it. All thanks to Charles and his group. How can you argue against the very agenda you were pushing without sounding like a flip-flopping asshole?"

The Ring of Fire and what to do about it had become the only issue that mattered to the Vampire Council and the Vampire Nation. There were two diametrically opposed schools of thought on the matter, and the vampire media had given names to both of them. On one side were *Progressionists* like Maurice, who wanted to expand vampiric existence through scientific and sociological means. On the other side were the far more numerous *Decimists*, whose quick and easy solution was the widespread decimation of humanity — the unleashing of vampire abilities that, in the minds of Decimists, had been held in check for too long. Decimists didn't care if they turned humans or killed them. They cared only about improving the vampire/human ratio.

One popular Decimist video showed Charles in a faked speech, ranting, "The Deacon got what he wanted. Prejudicial barriers have been removed! Anyone can become a vampire! We will accept all takers! And yet he's still not happy!"

Maurice had watched the video while slowly shaking his head. He wasn't any good at politics because he wasn't gifted at manipulation. On the surface, it looked as if Maurice had gotten what he wanted because anyone could be turned, but even a tiny bit of scrutiny revealed the difference between Maurice's vision of creative freedom and Charles's. Anyone could *become* a vampire, but only the elite were *remaining* vampires. Overweight, overly young, overly old, and disabled vampires were being staked as fast as they were created. Maurice didn't know the proper lie to tell in order to shift public attention from his seeming wishy-washiness and onto Charles's deception.

"It doesn't matter," said Maurice. "I'm still Deacon. I can't be assassinated outside of Council unless they want Gregor the Schizophrenic to take over. I can still veto laws through my proxy at Council. It's okay. I can live with being hated."

"You might want to adjust your complacency," said Reginald, whose mind had been entertaining daunting scenarios for weeks. "Gregor could be influenced, like a puppet, by Charles or someone like him. You could be assassinated on one of the trips you do take to Council. Decimists could simply take over the whole government in a coup, then reorganize it from top to bottom. Or what's going on now could simply keep happening — more reckless killings and turnings, done in the face of laws that nobody bothers to enforce. The law is a pretty fragile thing when you're the only one playing by its rules, Maurice."

"It doesn't matter," Maurice repeated, shrugging defiantly.

Celeste shot him an exasperated look, as if they'd discussed this over and over.

Nikki stood up. "How many people are dying, Maurice? How many people are being turned and being staked? It *does matter!*" Then she turned to

Reginald and said, "Tell him about the other thing."

Maurice looked at Reginald.

Reginald sighed and cocked his head to one side. "I'll just say this flat-out, without candy coating. Deacon Toussant, you're about to lose the small amount of power you still have."

"What do you mean?" said Maurice.

"Fangbook," said Reginald.

Maurice actually laughed. Fangbook was the vampire version of Facebook. Percentage-wise, Fangbook was actually far more popular and widespread than Facebook, with over eighty percent of American vampires using it at least once a month. Maurice considered the network stupid and frivolous, but a large percentage of the population felt differently.

Most vampires left behind a large group of family and friends□ when they were reborn. They could still interact with those people after turning, of course, but few did. A vampire's lifestyle wasn't entirely compatible with a human's, if for no other reason than because the latter was now considered food. So young vampires, suddenly blessed with amazing new abilities, found themselves without an outlet for their bragging and their stories of conquest, and Fangbook helped to fill that void. Fangbook friends became real friends. Because the vampire population was so much more spread out than the human population, newbie vampires tended to latch onto Fangbook as a discussion outlet for all of their darkest inner doings and desires rather than trying to find others in person. Fangbook was extremely explicit, and most users' photo sections looked like either police crime scene photos or porn shoots, and often both. The chat was wild and uninhibited. The network itself became a primary way to connect with other vampires, to form long-distance groups, and to arrange hunting parties or orgies.

"Don't laugh," Reginald continued. "Fangbook has over fifty-thousand users, and more each day as new vampires are created. You may not want to be a part of it, but most vampires do."

"So what? Let them whack off to murder photos and tell everyone else when they're reading the newspaper."

"Do you understand how it works?" said Reginald.

"More or less. Like a giant directory."

"That's what it used to be," said Reginald, "but it's more than that now. First of all, it connects eighty percent of the country's vampires — plus a lot of global vampires, though not as many — and it gives them a community. We're no longer loners living alone in holes, hiding from the daylight. Fangbook gives vampires a unified society and, as needed, a central place to discuss issues that matter to them so that everyone can participate. And do you know what they're discussing right now, and have been for months?"

"The Ring of Fire," said Nikki, pointing at Maurice like an accusation.

"And do you know *why* they're discussing it? Other than the fact that it's on their minds, I mean? Do you know *how* they're able to discuss it in such detail? Do you know how they're discussing facets of the *actual laws* on the table at Council?"

Maurice's forehead wrinkled. At least Reginald had his attention.

"There was a measure a while back, right?" said Maurice. "Something that opened records to the public or something."

"A simple thing," said Reginald. "The law you're talking about is now a few months old. All it did was to automatically post Council proceedings to the largest group on Fangbook. They already had permission to access that information, of course; it's all public record. But now, thanks to the new law, it started being dropped smack-dab in front of them on a regular basis. And that may sound like nothing, but what it's done is to keep the issue — in all of its legal, from-the-top detail — front and center in the collective psyche. People are very resilient and forgetful, and given time, they'd forget about the Ring of Fire and would get right back to everyday life. But this new measure ensures that they're presented with new information on a regular basis that will rile them up and remind them that the angels are watching all of us, that the clock is ticking, and that the Ring of Fire didn't go away. It just backed off a few paces, and could return at any time."

"And I didn't veto that measure," said Maurice.

"Well, it was a rider. It was tacked onto a bill that relaxed bootcamp admission requirements."

Reginald knew that Maurice would remember that one. He'd been excited when the Council had proposed expanding the group of humans eligible to become vampires. He'd taken it as a sign that his agenda and philosophy was slowly but surely getting through.

"So the populace is getting riled up," said Maurice. "And so... you think this puts me in more danger?"

"It does, yes. But there's more. Do you remember the Anti-Slaughter bill?"

Maurice nodded. The "Anti-Slaughter" bill was a measure that made it formally illegal to kill certain protected classes of humans. Maurice had been excited by that one as well. He thought it showed promise that the vampire psyche was becoming more empathetic.

"Do you remember the rider?"

This time, he shook his head.

"The rider on that bill was another very small thing. It allowed Fangbook users to 'Like' or 'Dislike' the Council information that was being pushed onto Fangbook. 'Liking' was already a big part of Fangbook. It's meaningless other than in Fangbook's algorithm, but basically, it indicates the popularity of certain posts. Popular posts and pages and whatever else get promoted, and unpopular ones fester and go away. What the rider did was to officially allow 'Liking' on laws. It didn't seem like much, except that laws proposed at Council that the Fangbook community liked the most rose to the top and were discussed more, and proposals that they didn't like were ditched."

Maurice watched Reginald and waited for him to go on. He slowly set down his chalice of blood.

"Don't you see?" said Nikki, who'd already had this discussion with Reginald. "It makes the Fangbook community like a mock Council. They're voting laws in or vetoing them."

"So what?" said Maurice. "Let the losers play. It sounds about as harmful as fantasy football."

"Fangbook is big, Maurice. It represents the will of the entire Vampire Nation. As goes Fangbook, so goes public opinion as a whole. Every time they vote a law up and you strike it down, you're pissing off eighty percent of the vampires in this country. Every time an unpopular law sneaks through, thanks to friends like Brian on the Council, you're pissing off eighty percent of the vampires in this country."

Maurice held his palms up in a *So what?* gesture.

"Fifty thousand people who decided to stop being humans and become immortal hunters and killers are worth being afraid of. Fifty thousand people who think it's fun and cool to post photos of themselves dismembering people."

Reginald felt sick. Spelling it all out was giving him a headache. Or maybe it was so much pot pie and cheesecake.

"I made a mistake, Maurice," he said.

Maurice looked over, his finger tracing circles lazily around the rim of his chalice.

Reginald kept his head down. He was supposed to be the brilliant one. Reginald had solved the Council relocation algorithm. Reginald had outsmarted the Council and overthrown its old leader. Reginald could read a whole book in seconds and had an encyclopedic memory of everything he'd ever experienced, nearly from birth until present, spanning both his vampire and human lives. He wasn't supposed to make simple mistakes, but he had.

Months ago, when he, Nikki, and Maurice had masterminded the overthrow of Logan, the Vampire Nation's previous Deacon, Nikki had still been human, and she'd pretended to be a vampire. She'd been armed only with dime store fangs, some flash powders, and her wits, and she'd told Reginald how terrified she'd been that the Guard would see right through her. They'd know she was human. They'd either kill her on the spot, or drink her dry.

They will see what they want to see, he'd told her. *That's the blindness of those at the top of the food chain. The predator is the one with guile. Nobody expects the prey to have guile, but a smart sheep will outsmart a blind wolf any day of the week.*

Time after time, Reginald had relied on the arrogance of others above him on the food and command chains to save him. He was fat. He was weak. He was slow. How could poor old Reginald ever be a threat to those big, bad vampires? But this time, *he'd* been the blind one. This time, *he'd* been on top, sitting by the Deacon's side in a position of power. This time, Charles and the Council had been the ones under someone's thumb, like subservient sheep. And like any smart, wily underdog, the Council had pulled a fast one by doing exactly the opposite of what the top dog expected.

"You made a mistake?"

"I thought Charles and the Council wanted power. I thought they wanted to find a way to overthrow you, so I watched carefully for power-grabbing legislation. But then I re-read the text of last week's Council activity the other day, and I realized that I'd missed something — a clever ploy that voluntarily *diminished* the Council's power."

"What are you talking about?"

Reginald looked up.

"Council passed a new law. It slipped right under our noses, just as it was designed to do. The law does not in any way reduce the power of the Deacon, but instead greatly reduces the power of the Council. Specifically, it limits the Council's power to that of *proposing* laws, and gives the power for *voting* on laws entirely over to the populace, instead of to the Council."

"So?"

"Specifically, it gives Council's old voting power to the only collective representation of the Nation's will that exists: Fangbook 'Likes' now tally up as votes. The language is very simple. It says that the Council proposes, and that the decision whether to make that proposal into a law is decided entirely by Fangbook."

"And my veto power?"

"Your veto power is over the Council's decisions. You have no dominion over Fangbook's decisions."

Maurice's shoulders rose and fell. He was watching something on the table that Reginald couldn't see, or that didn't exist.

"So the office of Deacon now means nothing, as far as voting is concerned."

"That's right. This change means that you're now just a symbolic figure. You're like the queen."

Maurice picked up his chalice while holding his pinky out, like the queen sipping tea. He made little old lady noises. Nikki watched him, not laughing. Nobody thought it was funny, so Maurice put the chalice down.

"So we need to appeal to the masses," said Maurice. "We've become a democracy. Is that terrible?"

"Yes," said Nikki and Reginald at the same time.

Maurice already knew that, of course. The Vampire Nation didn't track approval ratings on its Deacon, but if it had, Maurice's would be under fifteen percent by Reginald's calculation. Most of the young Nation considered him a throwback with ideas that were old and unhip. They considered him reactionary, and many considered him a sellout. They didn't like Reginald any better — partially because he'd dethroned a Deacon who in the eyes of most had greatly improved the standards and quality of the Nation's population, and partly because he was such an embarrassment to their kind. The loose coalition of busybodies that functioned as the vampire media easily swayed public opinion against him, against Maurice, and against all that they represented. It was common belief that Maurice's and Reginald's actions were what had brought on the wrath of the angels in the first place, leading to the species-threatening "Ring of Fire" detente that existed currently. It would be impossible for any of them to rally public support... and right now, all that terrified public wanted to do was to kill and turn until their angel overlords came down to pat them on their heads and tell them that they'd done a good job.

"They can do anything now," said Maurice.

"Yes," said Reginald, "they can."

MISSING

DINNER — IF THAT'S WHAT IT was called when four vampires drank blood while another gorged himself on pie — concluded on a mediocre note.

As was Maurice's tendency, he quickly dismissed the implications of the Council's new "given away" power and began making jokes. Celeste tried to goad him into an appropriately doomed mood, but nobody had the energy to keep pace with Maurice's talent for apathy. He'd been alive for over two thousand years, and disinterest had gotten him this far. Nikki told everyone (after a suitable period of exasperation at the Deacon's juvenile behavior) that maybe Maurice was right, and that their worrying and feeling distraught tonight wasn't going to make any difference. Maurice, seeing victory, said something about going with the flow. Reginald was tired from eating an entire cheesecake.

So for the remaining time they had, Maurice insulted Charles's style and haircut and demeanor, all of which were easy targets, and wondered about the whereabouts of the incubus Altus, who'd vanished after it was revealed that he was ten-year-old Claire's father.

"Eleven-year-old, now," said Reginald. "She had a birthday last week."

Even though Reginald wasn't related to Claire, he *had* tried very hard to feed on her when they'd first met, and she *had* saved him from starvation by giving him a bloody steak, and she *had* been threatened repeatedly by vampires thanks to her association with Reginald, so they'd formed an odd kind of kinship. He really should have visited her before now, and probably should have gotten her a present. He made a mental note to do it as soon as possible. Tomorrow it was really more important to attend the Council meeting — seeing as the world was falling apart and all — but after that, it was Claire time for sure.

Before Reginald and Nikki left, leaving a margin large enough to get home before the sun rose (Maurice kept forgetting they had to drive due to Reginald's inability to run faster than a ten-minute mile), Nikki asked about her intense thirst.

"Reginald is right," said Maurice. "It's probably blood ties. Some vampires feel it more than others."

"But Reginald doesn't have blood lust. He only has lust for taquitos. And you don't seem to have much blood lust, either."

"Well," said Maurice, "My age plus the fact that I'm your maker's maker gives you a deep well of vampire history to draw from. You could be getting your hunger from any of those who are related to me. Blood isn't just about proximity on the family

46

tree. It's kind of like the random toss that happens with genes, so you never know who your blood will end up being close to. You might feel my maker's maker in your blood at the same strength as you'd feel Reginald... who you'll *always* feel in your blood, by the way, because he is your maker."

"I will also permit you to feel me directly," Reginald told Nikki, tossing his head seductively.

"I have a lot of brothers and sisters," said Maurice, and *they* all have progeny. Right now, most of those vampires are probably killing several humans a day, drinking them dry, fun stuff like that."

Nikki gave her head a slow, exasperated shake.

"You don't have to give in to the thirst, Nikki. You don't *need* more blood. It's not unlike being influenced by your mother's opinion of what you do with your life. You can feel those impulses, and you can be driven to thirst by them, but whether or not you indulge them is always up to you."

Nikki sighed. "I thought I was done with willpower and dieting."

"Or you can drink as you've been drinking, and nobody will judge you," Maurice added. "Believe me, sentiment has changed a lot over the years. For a while in my youth, it was considered normal and fashionable to chain humans up and farm them for blood. It seems horrid now, but at the time, it was simply considered normal, not unlike keeping a cow for its milk."

But Nikki wouldn't want to hear about giving in. Now that Maurice had told her that she could choose to accept or ignore her thirst, she'd fight tooth and nail against it. Nikki sought out difficult and counterculture things to do, just to do them. As a human, Nikki had never taken her needs as gospel. She disliked the idea that she was a slave to her body's need for sleep and food, so she routinely denied herself one or the other or both for extended periods of time, just to show her body and the world who was boss, and who was in control.

They went home and slept, and throughout the next early evening, Reginald watched as Nikki fought what seemed to be an unfathomable thirst.

"Jesus, Nikki," said Reginald. "This is hard to watch. Let me order you a pizza girl or something." He picked up the phone, but Nikki waved him away.

"Put that phone down."

"You're so clearly uncomfortable," he said. "A snack won't hurt."

Nikki had been pacing the room. She became a blur and appeared in front of Reginald, holding his shirt by the collar.

"*Stop. Enabling. It,*" she said.

Then, as if snapping out of a trance, she blinked, gave her head a small shake, and let go of Reginald's collar as if she hadn't realized she'd been holding it.

"I'm sorry," she said, and resumed pacing.

48

Reginald wanted to tell her that what she'd just done proved just how on edge she was and argue that she should at least top herself off, but she would almost certainly take it the wrong way. As much as she loved Reginald, she hated his lack of restraint. "Just one more won't hurt" could have been carved on Reginald's tombstone, back when he might someday have needed one.

"If I give in, I'll just be feeding it," she said. "If I hold out, I can break it. Like a fast. After you fast for a while, you stop being hungry as you begin to master your body."

And that's why she did the things she did, he knew. *Control.*

Nikki had lived a life in which she'd had very little control. Her parents had both committed suicide, she'd been raised by a somewhat disinterested extended family, and she'd fallen into a directionless existence before finding Maurice in her teens. Her whole life, up into her twenties, had been spent in a tailspin. The main reason she'd dedicated years to vampire training had probably been because she wanted to know what it felt like to finally hold the reins. Fasting and sleep deprivation were just two more ways in which she proved that she wasn't willing to be at the unquestioned will of anything for long.

Reginald shrugged and opened a bag of Cheetos. Then he proposed a game of chess to give Nikki something to focus on other than her thirst, and she goaded him the whole time about how he'd rather play chess with his hot girlfriend than have sex with her. So he proposed having sex, and she laughed at him because he actually said "propose," and then the idea got lost and so they played chess, and Reginald let her win, as he did about a quarter of the time.

Before they knew it, it was time to head to their scheduled rendezvous with the Vampire Council Escorts. Maurice arrived at Reginald's house, and all three piled into Reginald's car for the trip.

The pickup spot was on the Ohio State University campus, behind a defunct bagel deli. Nikki couldn't stop talking, so she repeatedly expressed her reservations about putting herself in the hands of the Council, seeing as it was standard to be blindfolded and bound when in transit.

"You've just become powerless," she said to Maurice. "They can kill you the minute we arrive, because they all hate you and have hated you for forever, and because it no longer matters anymore who succeeds you as Deacon. Or they might kill *us*," she said, gesturing at herself and Reginald. "Maybe now, they can do it openly, because Fangbook said it was so."

"There's been no new legislation, and nothing more ominous than usual on Fangbook," said Reginald.

He'd stayed up and read the past six months of Council proceedings several times during the last day, and he'd spent hours analyzing traffic and sentiment across all areas of Fangbook having anything whatsoever with the Council, with the Ring of Fire, or with Deacon Toussant and his fat sidekick. He'd studied with an angry scowl on his face. The way the net had been cast over Maurice made Reginald feel like he'd failed, which of course he had. He had the best strategic mind in recent vampire history, but that hadn't stopped the Council from driving right through his blind spot.

"They'll kill us," said Nikki, pacing the small alley. The wall on one side was a solid red, with a huge black swath curling through its middle. It reminded Reginald of blood and doom.

"They're not going to kill us," said Reginald.

"How can you be sure?"

"I'm sure," he said quietly.

Maurice pulled his phone from his pocket, then looked around furtively. He looked very nervous.

"It's 12:02," he said.

Reginald stopped watching Nikki. His head snapped toward Maurice, then jerked around the small alley as if he thought he might simply have missed a huge black Council Escort SUV that had been there all along. All he saw were dumpsters and a battered Ford Tempo in a small alcove off of the alley, parked in front of a fire escape. He reached into his pocket and fished out his own phone. 12:02.

"You're sure the window was midnight?" said Maurice.

Reginald tapped his head, which was essentially the same as tapping a notarized copy of the official Council notice.

Maurice blurred from one end of the alley to the other. He appeared on the roof of the red-walled building and ran its perimeter, looking down. Then he appeared next to Reginald again and said, "Nothing. The streets are reasonably quiet. Where would they be coming from?"

"North," said Reginald, and gave Maurice the route the SUV would take. Maurice vanished in a cloud of dust and leaves, then reappeared thirty seconds later. "Nothing. The Escort is not coming."

Nikki sat heavily onto a discarded crate. Above her, hanging in the overhead electrical wires, was what looked like the skeleton of an annihilated corded wall phone. She looked paler than normal.

"What does it mean?" said Maurice.

Reginald felt a strange sensation of role-reversal. Maurice had been around since the day B.C. had become A.D. *He* was supposed to be the authority on vampires and vampire culture in this group — mentor to both his progeny, Reginald, and *his* progeny, Nikki. And here he was, asking Reginald what to do. The notion gave Reginald as much of a chill as the absence of the Council Escorts.

"I don't know," said Reginald.

They sat in silence, all of them waiting and hoping for the arrival of the vehicle they had been dreading moments earlier. Council Escorts were never late. *Never.* The entire American Vampire Nation's leadership ran like a giant, perfect clock. A master coded algorithm chose a new location for the Council every ten days, and then coordinated the relocation with scores of what were essentially vampire roadies. The Council was disassembled, moved, and reassembled, its parts shipped via dozens of different routes through dozens of different hands. Those coming into the Council were shuffled through multiple pairs of Escorts, none of which knew the whole of the route and all of which were wired with failsafe devices that triggered and killed them automatically if GPS tracking suggested that they'd gone rogue. Only the algorithm knew it all, and the algorithm was perfect. When you received word that your pickup window was between midnight and 12:30am, you could set your watch by the arrival of the Escort vehicle. The idea that it hadn't arrived and didn't seem likely to — not within the window, anyway — was disturbing beyond words. Paranoia was the one thing that the Council could be counted on to maintain even while everything else crumbled. What did cracks in the perfection of paranoia mean?

"What do we do now?" said Nikki.

She and Reginald looked at Maurice, but Maurice was already looking at Reginald, waiting for *him* to answer. Nikki turned to look at Reginald, waiting.

"How should I know?" said Reginald.

"You're the chess player," said Nikki. Something in her face said that she knew that she'd been allowed to win the games she'd won against Reginald.

"I don't know. We could go to the Council directly, instead of going through the Escorts."

Maurice's lip curled. Nobody was supposed to know where the Council was located at any given time — and as far as the Council knew, nobody did. But Reginald had cracked the algorithm almost a year ago, and could not only pinpoint the Council whenever he wanted, but could also roll its position back and forth through time as needed.

"You want to show your hand?" said Maurice. "You want to let them know you've cracked the algorithm?"

"I want to *go to the Council*," said Reginald. "Now more than ever. This bothers me. It's like the center is disintegrating."

"That's bad?" said Nikki.

"The farce of government is all that's keeping the Nation from outright chaos," said Reginald. "Remove that, and tens of thousands of terrified vampires will no longer have anyone to tell them how to react to things like the Ring of Fire. Most of them have already decided that what Balestro wanted was for them to kill and turn until half of the planet or more was vampire."

"That's bad," said Nikki.

"Where is the Council now?" said Maurice.

Reginald's eyes rolled up for a half-second. Nowadays, he didn't need to go to and read the algorithm as needed. He'd started carrying it around in his head.

"Outside of Polaris. North of 270." And he gave them an address.

Twenty minutes later, they piled out of Reginald's car. Nikki and Maurice sprinted in twin blurs toward the back door of a warehouse with a large FOR RENT sign out front. Finding the door chained from the outside, they circled the building, Nikki moving clockwise and Maurice moving counterclockwise. Reginald hadn't yet reached the building. He'd tried to sprint with Nikki and Maurice, had immediately started to run out of breath, and had tripped on a brick anchored at the head of a parking space.

"All doors are chained from the outside," said Maurice, joining the others.

"There must be another entrance. They wouldn't chain themselves in," said Reginald.

"Where?"

"Does it matter?" Nikki returned to the nondescript back door, placed a hand on the push bars of both doors, and gave a small shove. The door shuddered in its frame, then both doors wrenched completely free of their hinges with a sound like an explosion. The metal doors fell inward and clanged onto a dark concrete floor. Ironically, the chain between the doors held.

"Those are pull bars, not push bars," said Reginald.

"Oops," said Nikki, stepping over the felled doors and into the dark warehouse lobby.

"Totally dark," said Maurice. He vanished in a blur, and Nikki did the same. Reginald sat down on a box near the door and wiped blood off of his knee. He'd taken off a lot of skin when he'd tripped in the parking lot, and although the wound had healed instantly, there was a lot of blood. Reginald found that the sight of blood still made him queasy — a significant challenge to his new lifestyle.

Nikki appeared behind him, her ass barely on the tiny remaining amount of box that Reginald's formidable ass wasn't occupying. Several pieces of paper, caught in her slipstream, fluttered toward them. Reginald caught one. It said that the building's rent came with utilities paid and that the price had just been reduced. There was a photo in the corner of a very unattractive realtor whose name was apparently Floyd.

"The Council is not here," said Nikki. "You must have read it wrong."

"No," said Reginald patiently, "I didn't. Math is black and white. Right now, the algorithm places the Council here. Maybe there's a basement."

"They'd be up here," said Nikki.

Maurice appeared beside her. "Agreed. They'd use the main space. There aren't any basements in this industrial park, anyway. It's too near lowlands."

Reginald felt troubled. The Council, like its Guards and Escorts, was supposed to operate like clockwork. They couldn't have changed the algorithm. Nobody understood it well enough to change it. All they could do would be to restart it, and the logistics of doing so were bafflingly complex. Besides, he'd gotten the notice about their pick-up time window with the Escorts, so as of a few hours ago, everything was on track.□ Yet the Escorts hadn't arrived and Council was missing. What was going on? The only thing that bothered Reginald more than a secure, efficient Vampire Council was a sloppy or a missing one.

"What now?" said Maurice. Again deferring to Reginald as if he were senior. Reginald didn't like that, either.

"I don't know."

"Come on, Reginald. What now?"

He shrugged. "All I know to try is to go to where it was last. Although I don't know if I'll be happy or terrified if I find it destroyed." He was thinking of the two disasters at Council that had preceded their trip to Europe, to meet Balestro the angel at the stone altar in Germany. One of those times, the roof had been blown off of the Council and hundreds had died, the rest buried in rubble through the daylight hours. And even then, the Council had survived and moved on. The idea that another disaster might have occurred filled Reginald with foreboding.

"It's not destroyed unless it happened very recently," said Nikki.

"How do you know?" said Maurice.

"Fangbook."

"You're on Fangbook?"

"You're the only one who's *not* on Fangbook, Maurice," she said. "I even joined a group on out-of-control thirst. Some very good support to be had in there. But to answer your question, there would have been buzz if something had happened, but there hasn't. I even saw a status update from Charles."

" 'CHARLES BARKLEY... is being a dickbag,' " Maurice read off of an imaginary Fangbook status update.

Reginald shook his head.

"Contact the Council," said Maurice. "Tell them the Escorts didn't show. Ask for a new window."

Reginald was still shaking his head. "I don't like it. It's not by the book, and 'by the book' is all the Council knows."

Reginald stood up, picking at his shredded and bloody pantleg, and began walking back toward the car. Nikki and Maurice followed. Reginald climbed into the drivers' seat, then made an annoyed noise and moved the seat all the way back, to switch from Maurice-driving mode to Reginald-driving mode. In the back seat, Maurice moved to the opposite side, sitting behind Nikki.

"Where are we going?" said Maurice.

"Back to campus, where we just were," said Reginald. "And when we get there, if we find what I think we'll find, I'm going to punch the Council members in the face."

"Why?"

"Because I get terrible gas mileage on this car, and someone owes me gas money," said Reginald.

He shoved the transmission into gear and the car lurched forward, back past Polaris and toward the expressway.

COUNCIL

THEY FOUND THE VAMPIRE COUNCIL where the algorithm had left it two weeks earlier — in a cavernous and forgotten space beneath a club on High Street called the Asbury.

They'd parked the car less than two blocks from where they'd initially waited for the Escorts and walked a few blocks, through campus streets and alleyways, until they'd come to the front of the club. Posters in the entryway advertised coming bands. There was a very large man in the ticket booth wearing sunglasses. He was asleep. Maurice walked into the ticket booth, kicked the man, and got no response. Then he reached down and pulled up the man's lip to reveal a slightly-sharper-than-normal canine tooth that would descend into a fang for feeding.

"He's not asleep," said Maurice. "He's drunk."

"Vampires can get drunk?" said Reginald. He couldn't believe the issue had never come up, either in his own experience or in anything he'd read. But then, neither Reginald nor Nikki were really drinkers, and neither was terribly social outside of their own circle of three.

"Not like humans." Maurice kicked the man again. "We don't metabolize alcohol. But what we

60

can metabolize is the blood of a human who's been drinking a lot. And I'll tell you something: someone this size would have to drain three or four totally shitfaced humans to get drunk enough to pass out."

Maurice pushed on a small door at the back of the ticket booth. From where Reginald was standing, he could see blood on the back wall of the smaller chamber it revealed and what was either the top of a bald head or something that looked like one.

"Humans like these fine folks here, for instance," said Maurice, re-closing the door and exiting the ticket booth. He shook his head. "That's so sloppy. So flagrant. Bodies tossed into a closet like empty whiskey bottles. What's going to happen on Friday, when college students pour in here to buy tickets to see whatever band is playing?"

Nikki stood on her toes, bringing her higher off the ground even than her ill-advised heels, and peered into the ticket booth. There was blood everywhere — on the counter, on the floor, down the unconscious vampire's shirt.

"This is a Guard?"

"Probably a lookout." Maurice opened the door again. "Lookout!" he yelled, then kicked the vampire hard in the groin. He re-closed the door.

"What's going on here?" said Nikki.

"I think the shit might be hitting the fan."

Reginald was nodding. "This makes sense."

"It *does*?"

"I'll show you later. Let's just say that what's been coming out of Council lately has been less professional but more honest than usual. Come on."

Reginald led them through the lobby and into the main hall, which looked large in its emptiness. There was a stage across the room bordered by black curtains. Above the stage was a rack of can lights covered with multicolored gels, and further back were several larger spotlights. A shallow sunken dance area with a wood or laminate floor was in front of the stage, and the pit was surrounded by a slightly higher level floor studded with tables. Nobody appeared to be present.

To the left of the stage, past the pit, was a door that looked like it might cover a stairwell. A large red EXIT sign was above the door, but the door was ajar and Reginald could see a corridor of some sort beyond it. Above the door, a boxy pneumatic closer had been broken away from the door and hung against it, limp.

"There," said Reginald, pointing. "Council will be downstairs, through that door. There *should* be at least two uniformed Guard at the top of the staircase, then more at the bottom. The door should, of course, be latched and locked, and it should open on a thumbprint. But look: it's as secure as Grandma's broken screen door."

Reginald, at the head of the trio, walked over and pulled the door open. Without the closer attached, the door swung wide with no resistance and banged against the facing wall. Then it stayed that way, hanging open like a yokel's slack jaw. From the stairwell came the sounds of a large gathering, maybe even a party.

Reginald looked at Maurice, whose face bore an expression somewhere between trepidation and fury. His fangs had descended, and his nineteen-year-old's eyes looked as steely as a demon's. He was embarrassed to be a vampire if this was what it meant to be one, and he wanted to make someone pay for that feeling.

Reginald patted the air to tell Maurice to calm down, then did the same to Nikki. Losing control would only make a bad situation worse. But it was hard; Reginald himself felt his ire rising. There was no love lost between Reginald, Maurice, Nikki, and the Vampire Council, but until now, their acrimonious relationship had at least held a kind of professional courtesy.

"Before we go further," he said, "before you let things get ugly, remember that this is still the Vampire Council, and that you are still its Deacon."

Maurice forced his mouth closed, but Reginald could tell from the fullness of his upper lip that his fangs hadn't retracted. When he spoke, they got in his way like a pair of dime store fakes.

"I am nothing," said Maurice. "You said it yourself."

"You still hold some sway, even if it's just symbolic," said Reginald.

"I could kill them all."

"Okay," said Reginald. He took a step forward and patted his maker on the back. "Let's call that Plan B. Come on."

Reginald allowed Maurice to take the lead as they walked down the steps and into the basement. He had no idea what to expect, and Maurice was stronger than he was by several orders of magnitude. Nikki took up the rear, and Reginald was sandwiched in the middle. The party sounds increased as they descended. Reginald heard howls, hoots, and music. It was like walking into a biker bar. And maybe that's what they were doing, he thought... except that there was a drunk vampire upstairs, and several dead humans in a closet.

What they found at the bottom of the basement steps was closer to Council than a biker bar, but not by much.

Once inside the Council complex — which was disassembled and reassembled each time the location changed — individual Councils were supposed to be indistinguishable from each other. The walls were always white. There was always an entrance corridor, then a foyer area with several pure white holding cells. Beyond the cells was supposed to be a short corridor into a packed dirt arena surrounded by rows of seats. Inside of this arena, the Council box was always to the left. The

Deacon's box was always higher, always more or less in the center. There were, ever since the first Council catastrophe, always a ring of sniper windows at the top edge of the arena room from which Guards could fire wooden bullets, and the room itself always had a high roof, which limited the locations in which the complex could be assembled. To the far left side of the arena was a door that opened into a silo-like room. The roof of this room that could be opened to the sun for executions. The current meetingplace was underground, so the sun would be indirect (reflected from the surface via several large mirrors), but the room was always there, and the ceiling always retracted to let in the sun.

What they found when they reached the complex at the foot of the stairs was roughly correct. There was an entrance hall, a foyer with cells, and an arena. But beyond those basics, the Council was a mess. The arena, formed by composite walls made to resemble stone, looked battered and beaten. There were large gaps in the walls through which Reginald could see the rock of the underground cavern beyond. Vampires were milling everywhere, as if the place were a vast open market. The activity in itself was odd. Council was normally quiet at night, because meetings occurred during the day. Yet here they were, hours before dawn, still awake and at full throttle.

As Reginald, Nikki, and Maurice made their way through the crowd, Reginald realized that many of those they passed were humans, not vampires. He could smell them. Humans, unlike vampires, had a coppery odor, like blood. Their musk traveled into his nose, down the back of his throat, and landed on his tongue, like a penny.

Most of the humans were complicit, moving docilely under the guidance of their vampire escorts. Others were clearly glamoured — slim businessmen in their suits, their throats red and sore, women who looked bedraggled and bruised. An ad-hoc corral even seemed to have been erected in the corner of the arena out of boxes. Glamoured humans milled in the small, triangular area. Despite the fog of glamour, Reginald could still see fear in many of their eyes — an uncertain, stupid kind of fear, like an animal's — and Reginald reminded himself that not every vampire was as talented at mental manipulation as he was.

They found the massive figure of Brian Nickerson in the Council chamber. Brian rose to greet them with his arms out and a smile on his face. He wrapped his arms around all three of them in a giant bear hug. Then, after a squeeze, he stepped back and put his hands on his hips.

"Well!" he said, looking each of them over in turn. "It's been a while. How have you been? Nikki! Vampirism looks great on you. It's like you were made for this."

Brian had met Nikki before, but hadn't seen her since she'd become a vampire. Nikki the vampire had a totally different bearing than Nikki the human. She was still the same person, but she looked as if she'd been run through several sharpening filters. She was tighter and harder in appearance and manner. She was one of those people who really had become Herself 2.0 when she was turned.

Brian was still smiling, his hands still on his hips. He looked like he was greeting his kid back home after a long first year in college.

"Brian?" said Maurice. He was looking at Brian as if he had three heads.

"Yessir."

"What's happened here?"

Brian flapped a hand as big as a ham. "Oh, it's a slippery slope around here lately. I just try to ignore these assholes. I mostly read and surf the internet. Wired internet, of course, and only on the protected network. You still can't get a cellular or GPS signal in here. You have to go up top for that, onto High Street."

Reginald felt a headache beginning. The reason cellular signals were jammed in Council was because nobody on the inside was supposed to be able to ascertain their location. The Council was intended to be a black box — you were brought in blindfolded via a series of Escorts, and once in the compound, you couldn't leave until you were sent out blindfolded via a series of Escorts. The fact that the Council structure was always exactly the same meant that whether the Council was located at the top of a mountain or under a river, the experience was always identical. But this casual location awareness? This casual coming and going? The fact that the Escorts hadn't shown had really only been the tip of the iceberg. The breaches of security Reginald was seeing were indicative of a system-wide breakdown.

"When did your Escort bring you in?" asked Brian.

"They didn't," said Maurice. "The Escort didn't show, so we went to where Council was supposed to be — something Reginald has been able to figure out for months. When it wasn't there, he looked back in time to where you were supposed to be last. We walked in past a drunk lookout and through an open door, into the complex. We didn't see any Escorts. Or, for that matter, any Guard."

"You saw them," said Brian, apparently nonplussed by the fact that Reginald had broken the Council algorithm. "They're just never where they're supposed to be anymore, and they don't usually wear their helmets. They kind of do what they want, when they want, and beat people when it suits them." He leaned against one of the prefab walls, which wasn't properly anchored and buckled under his weight.

"Why didn't you tell us that this was happening?" said Maurice.

"I sent you a Fangbook message," said Brian.

"I don't use Fangbook," said Maurice.

"Ah," said Brian, as if the whole thing was just a minor inconvenience. "Well, everyone has an account whether they use it or not. I didn't realize. Don't worry; I would have figured out after a while that you didn't get it. But most of this —" He waved his hand in an all-encompassing gesture "— has happened since the last time we were supposed to move. What was that... a week ago?"

"Two days."

"Ah. Well, time flies."

Maurice walked up to stand very close to Brian. Brian absolutely dwarfed Maurice, but Maurice radiated some of his millennia of age and his superior strength as he said, "More slowly this time, Brian... *what happened here?*"

"The people who don't like you realized that the emperor has no clothes," said Brian. He began to pick his teeth with a fingernail. Brian was on their side, but he was also infuriatingly unperturbable. He tended to go with the flow even when the flow was going somewhere intensely stupid.

"Fangbook," said Nikki, as if the word were an obscenity.

Brian nodded. "Yeah, it's a bitch when public opinion is so obviously, visibly, unanimously against you. Charles gave a big speech once that last measure passed — the *last* big speech; can't believe it was as recent as it must've been — and said that the Vampire Nation was finally out from under the thumb of oppression, as if you'd been Stalin. He didn't mention how your 'thumb' and your 'oppression' was a significant reprieve from two hundred years under Logan. It was quite an intelligent speech, for Charles. I remember wondering if he'd had a speechwriter. He talked about returning power to the people... democracy and all of that. It went over very well. You should see the video on his Fangbook page. It's got like a gazillion Likes. But the thing is, it's not as if anything you see *here* — with all of the stupidity out in the arena and the Guards dicking off and whatnot — was open to a vote. It just kind of happened. People started saying, 'Let's try something and see if anyone stops us.' The first people to do it were the Guards, who've hated serving you since day one, and nobody was going to stop them, because who's going to guard the Guards? And when nothing happened and the Guards just kind of got away with ignoring their duties, other people began to try things. Fast forward a few days, and..." Brian shrugged.

"And the Council's missed relocation?" said Reginald.

"Another set of orders that nobody felt like obeying all of a sudden, in our newly democratized paradise. Once the perimeter was breached and they realized that they were below a bar, they started bringing down liquor, just out of human habit. When the liquor didn't get them drunk, they started harvesting humans and bringing them down here to get *them* drunk. That's how it's been since. If the humans catch on before feeding-slash-getting-drunk time, someone glamours them or kills them. There's a subbasement below this one.

Don't go down there if you find it. It's filled with empties."

"Bottles?" said Nikki.

"Bodies," said Brian.

Maurice's face was twisting, contorting, becoming ugly. Suddenly something snapped and he thrust both of his hands into Brian's massive chest. Brian was four times Maurice's size, but he went through the wall as if he were a stone and the wall were a brittle window. He annihilated the partitions and the metal reinforcements behind them as he went, then broke a star shape into the basement's rock wall. Dust puffed from around Brian as he came to a stop.

Brian's hand went to the back of his head and came away with a pool of blood on the palm. He shook the blood off, wiped his red hand on his pants, and probed the back of his head to make sure the wound had knitted before brushing himself off and standing up.

"Damn, Maurice." Still unperturbed. His fangs weren't even out, but Maurice's were, and he was walking forward, through the hole, toward Brian.

"How could you let this happen?" Maurice growled.

"How could *you* let this happen?"

The expression fell off of Maurice's face as if it were hot. His fangs vanished.

"This is all legal, Maurice. There's no law requiring Escorts and Guards to maintain Council security. It's protocol, but it's not law. And as for abducting humans? Legal. *Killing* humans? Legal. Fraternizing? Legal. And if you, as Deacon, had something to say about all of it? Well, it's now totally legal to ignore you, and to put whatever stupid idea they have up to a public vote. So if you were so goddamn concerned about the way Council was conducting itself, maybe you should have attended a meeting or two instead of sending your idiot proxy every damn time and ignoring us."

Brian, finally perturbed, brushed the last of the basement dust off of his pants and squeezed through the hole, back into the Council chamber. Once inside, he looked at the hole in the otherwise pristine wall, frowned, and then walked across the room to fetch a large bookcase to place in front of it. He gave it an approving nod and said, "Better."

Maurice fell into a chair, his anger deflated.

"This is about fear," said Reginald, stepping in front of him.

Maurice looked up.

"It looks sloppy, and it looks defiant, and it looks murderous and bloodthirsty. But it's all happening because the vampires here — and the vampires out there, in the rest of the country and the world — are *terrified*. This is a ship without a captain. They're doing what feels best because nobody is telling them what to do." Reginald nudged Maurice. "You've got a society of hunters and murders on the verge of chaos, starting from the top down. I suggest you get out there and be the captain, if you still can."

"I don't know where to begin explaining how futile that is," said Maurice.

Reginald stooped down so that his face was even with Maurice's. "Nobody wants you to lead, and everyone hates you. *But you are still the Deacon of this Nation.* Stop feeling sorry for yourself and ask yourself two questions: One, what will happen if *nobody* leads? And two, who will lead if *you* don't?"

Over Reginald's shoulder, Brian Nickerson said, "That reminds me. There's something else we should talk about."

Reginald stood and waited for Brian to continue.

"There's been talk about a duly-elected president."

"That's good, right?" said Nikki.

Brian shrugged. "So far, there's only one obvious candidate..."

"Wait," said Reginald, who saw the punchline coming.

"... and that would be Councilman Charles Barkley," said Brian.

LITTLE MERLIN

CLAIRE CAME OUT OF THE church she went to after school to find Reginald balancing on a fencepost on one leg, his other leg up, and his arms over his head in a crane kick posture. Reginald was glad she came out when she did, because the fencepost was starting to buckle. The fence itself was chain link, but Reginald didn't know if the fenceposts for chain link fences were sunk in concrete or not.

Claire took one sidelong glance at Reginald and kept walking. It was ten o'clock, and the streetlights had been on for a while. She made it all the way into the cone of light beneath one of them before turning back around to let Reginald, who thought she'd missed him, off the hook.

"I saw you," she told Reginald. "I was just ignoring you."

Reginald hopped down and scampered over to her. "Thank God. You commit to a joke like that, and you end up in character forever. I've been balancing on that post for like ten minutes."

"Good thing you're a vampire and don't feel pain."

"I *heal*," he said. "But I still feel pain."

They walked a bit further along the sidewalk, content.

"That was Daniel-san from *The Karate Kid*. The famous crane kick move," said Reginald, gesturing back at the fence.

"It's cute, your balance ability," she said. "But is it at all useful? Like in a fight?"

"Sure it is. I can crane kick my opponents."

Claire giggled.

"Then I can do wax on and wax off." He put his palms out in front of himself and made circles in the air as if he were waxing a car. The rhythmic motion made his gut jiggle.

Claire giggled again, then pulled gloves from her pockets and put them on. Her hood was already up. She said, "Seriously."

"Seriously, it's useless," he said. "But you just wait a thousand years, when I finally get some vampire speed and strength. Then I'll be able to dodge bullets like in *The Matrix*. I'll be able to walk on my hands along tiny ledges and run across tightropes. I'll be like Fat Spiderman."

This time, she didn't laugh.

They were nearing Claire's house. If Claire's mother Victoria was home, Claire would invite Reginald inside, and he and Claire would sit on the couch while Victoria brought them Rice Krispie treats. Reginald had no idea why it was always Rice Krispie treats, because he hadn't implanted any such suggestion in Victoria when he'd perma-glamoured her into forever believing that Reginald was her brother. Nikki said that maybe it was some kind of buried motherly instinct, like from the caveman days. Reginald said that cavemen didn't have Rice Krispies, and Maurice, for his part, said that it was all crap because there was no such thing as perma-glamouring. But Victoria brought him treats and tried to invite him to family reunions, so what did Maurice know?

"Hey," said Reginald, nudging Claire with his elbow. "Happy birthday."

"Thanks."

"I got you a present." He handed her a small wrapped package that was about the size of a box of wooden kitchen matches. It was wrapped in pink paper and tied with a red bow. Claire stopped under a streetlight to unwrap it and then smiled a genuine, little-girl smile at what she found. She removed the contents of the box and shoved it into her mouth, then tucked the box into the pocket of her coat.

"Thanth, Wegi-ald," she said, grinning at him with gigantic, ivory white fangs.

"They're for adults," he said. "You may need to grow into them. Honestly, I counted myself lucky to find porcelain fangs at all, but the plastic ones are crap. Just ask Nikki."

"Doww I feew vihthus," said Claire. Then she pulled the fangs from her mouth, returned them to the box, and slid the box into her pocket. "I need to work on my enunciation," she explained.

"Wear them in good health," said Reginald. They continued walking in silence until they reached her front door. She opened it, walked inside, and closed the door.

Reginald, still outside, knocked. When Claire opened the door, she found that he had turned so that his back was facing into the house. He said, "Have you seen my awesome moonwalk?" and began taking steps backward. An invisible wall of force pushed back, making him walk in place.

"Sorry," said Claire. "Come in."

Unsupported once the spell broke, Reginald fell into the foyer. When he got up, he found that Claire had walked into the kitchen. He closed the front door and walked down the hall to join her. There was an island in the middle of the kitchen, and tall stools stood around the island. Reginald sat in one, his ass spilling over all of its edges. Claire was making herself a peanut butter and jelly sandwich.

"Do you know that it's coming up on a year since I first tried to kill you?" he said.

"You don't have it in you to kill anyone," said Claire. The way she said it, it was as if there was a double-meaning, but Reginald wasn't catching it. He could read adults well, but kids were hard. Probably because so little of what kids did made rational sense, or possibly because everything they did made much more sense than the things that adults did.

"Since I tried to drink your blood, then."

Claire half smiled. "Looking back, now that you've had real blood, how bad was the steak I gave you?"

"Well," said Reginald. "It was no Cheesecake Factory turtle cheesecake."

Claire looked at where Reginald was looking, then rolled her eyes. "Oh, that's subtle. Would you like me to offer you a piece?" She pulled the door of the refrigerator back open.

"That'd be fantastic if you offered me a piece."

"Would you like a piece?"

"That'd be fantastic." And he patted the place in front of him on the island, licking his lips. Then, after she'd placed a small plate in front of him, laden with two pieces of cheesecake, he asked if her mother was home.

Claire looked at the clock. "Should be soon. She had a thing that ended at ten, just a few miles away."

Reginald watched Claire while he ate his cheesecake, while she ate her sandwich.

"What's up, Claire?"

"Hmm?"

"You didn't laugh at Daniel-san on the fencepost or any of my other hilarious jokes. You seem distracted. Old age getting to you?"

Claire took a deep breath, held it, and then exhaled. "If I ask you a question, you'll be straight with me, won't you?"

Reginald nodded slowly.

"All this stuff that's happening on the news. It's vampires, isn't it?"

Well, he'd promised. "Yes."

Claire shook her head.

"You've got an order of protection," said Reginald. "You and your mom both." But something felt wrong in his throat as he said it. It felt like lying, and then he realized that it was, in a way. The Council was ignoring its simplest mandates. The Council was allowing wanton creation of new vampires, which was the very charge that Reginald had almost been executed for. What were the chances that anyone would obey an order of protection that had been issued by the Deacon they'd just made irrelevant?

"This is it, though, isn't it?" said Claire.

Reginald almost laughed. It was essentially the question he'd come here to ask.

"The what?"

"The war."

"The one you predicted?"

Claire rolled her eyes. They'd had this conversation before. When Balestro had threatened to destroy all of the world's vampires, Reginald had revealed his ace-in-the-hole: Claire, whose absentee father turned out to be Altus the incubus. The only other known incubus-human hybrid had been a powerful wizard named Merlin, but Claire, who bluffed her way through the Balestro encounter, maintained that she had no prescience whatsoever.

"My dad was a trucker. Not an incubus," said Claire.

"Altus is your father. I'm sorry, kiddo, but it's true. Balestro knew it was true."

"Then why don't I *know* anything? Why don't I have any powers? Why can't I shoot lightning and give fortunes? I'm just a normal girl! A *sub*-normal girl, who gets picked on because she's small and poor!"

Reginald made a face, ready to protest, but Claire waved it away. Slowly, she got herself under control and then said, "What about you, huh? Anything come of that lightning bolt he hit you with?"

"Maybe it was a warning," said Reginald, shrugging.

"You told me afterward that he'd 'given you something.'"

"Maybe he 'gave me' a cold," said Reginald.

Claire punched his arm.

"Seriously, I don't know!" said Reginald, feigning injury and rubbing his arm. "If you can be a wizard who doesn't know her powers, I can be a vampire an angel hit with a lightning bolt who has no idea what he's received. I don't feel any different. I don't have any new powers. At the time, all I had was a headache, and now that's gone."

"Maybe our secret powers will show up when we both hit puberty," said Claire.

Reginald ate his cheesecake. Claire ate her sandwich. The kitchen was almost too quiet, but Claire's house was always quieter than it seemed like it should be. The houses on both sides were now vacant, and Claire's mother was bewitched into quiet submission whenever Reginald was around.

When the food was finished, Claire smiled a tight-lipped smile at Reginald and shrugged. The gesture said, *What now?*

"I got you another present," said Reginald. He was wearing a small shoulder bag. He pulled a rectangular package out of it and handed it to Claire. She unwrapped it and gushed.

"*Columbo* on DVD!" she hooted. Reginald couldn't help but feel her contagious enthusiasm. Neither Reginald nor Claire would have had any use for *Columbo* if he'd never tried to feed on her, but ever since they'd met and Claire had become a kind of surrogate child to Reginald, *Columbo* had been something they shared.

Claire slid the first disc into the player and pressed Play.

"Claire, I'd like you to try to stay inside after dark from now on, okay?" he said. "Your mom too. Seeing as you're the daughter of an incubus and all, I won't try to lie to you..." He made mystical gestures around her head, but she didn't smile. "... but there's been a lot of upset at the Council. The upshot is that I don't know that you can count on that order of protection."

"They won't kill me," said Claire. "I'm Merlin."

"Just the same," said Reginald.

Five minutes passed.

"You really are, you know," he said.

The intervening five minutes made the comment totally out of place. Claire looked over at him as if he had two heads.

"You really are something like Merlin, I mean. Your mother is human. Your father is an incubus. You may not know that you can see the future, but I'll bet you can."

Claire looked over, then paused the DVD. She studied Reginald and then, quite suddenly, a knowing smile exploded onto her face. Reginald knew he was about to be mocked, but that was okay because she looked genuinely happy.

"You came here to ask me something!" she said. "You did, you did!" She swapped her giddy expression for a serious one, then bowed her head reverently and put her hands together as if in prayer. "What can the master assist you with, my son?"

"Play the DVD," said Reginald.

"Come on, champ!" she said. "You're trying to be all cool now because I've already told you I can't see anything, but you came here to ask my advice. Ha! I'm eleven. You guys are hundreds or thousands of years old and all-powerful, and you want *me* to tell you what to do!"

"I'm thirty-eight," said Reginald.

"What's the issue? Come on. Give."

So Reginald sighed, prepared for mockery, and explained the changes at Council to Claire. She'd already been through two major vampire crises, so he went ahead and told her everything: the changes in the law that made Maurice irrelevant and powerless, the crumbling of the Council, the lawlessness and threat of chaos and the human decimation it would probably bring with it, and the promise of a democratically elected president in Sir Charles.

"Oh, it won't be *that* knob," said Claire. Then the dismissive smile vanished from her face and she looked shocked.

"Really?"

"I was just saying. Nobody would vote for that guy."

Now Reginald was the one who was smiling. "No, that's not what you were saying at all. You just blurted that out. Do it again."

"You think I'm predicting the future?"

"I kind of do. When I was learning to read like a vampire, it felt like it was taking me hours to read books that I'd actually read in seconds. Then, when Maurice asked me about what I'd read — like really detailed, minutia-type questions — I didn't think I knew the answers... but then I did. Maurice said it was like using a muscle on a limb you didn't know you had. Just now, you surprised yourself with that answer. I'll bet I showed the same surprise at first."

But Claire shook her head and, no matter how much Reginald goaded her, wouldn't say more.

Reginald looked at the clock. Claire saw where he was looking, and her eyes went to the front door. She said, "What?"

"Nothing."

"Reginald, *what?*"

"Just... no worries, okay? But when did you say your mom was supposed to be home?"

"Maybe a few minutes after ten." Her eyes went back to the clock. It was twenty after. She looked at Reginald, the door, the clock. Her mouth made an O.

"I'm sure she's just running late," he said.

"It's a work thing. She would't stay a minute longer than she had to."

"Then they held her up. Or she stopped to chat."

But Claire already looked panicked. There was almost certainly nothing to it, but she was worked up because he'd just told her about the recent lawlessness he'd seen downtown. And sure, vampires were killing, draining, and turning humans more and more in recent days, but just because Victoria walked alone in a neighborhood where even the police weren't surprised when people ended up missing didn't mean that...

"Okay, I'll check," he said. Then, because he felt as if he was essentially Claire's adopted father, added, "But *only* to set your mind at ease, because I've got to be going."

He stood up and trotted heavily toward the door. Claire was on his heels. When he reached the door, he turned around and told her that he'd be right back.

"I'm coming with you," said Claire.

"Like hell you are. Not that there's anything to be afraid of, of course, but because this neighborhood isn't a place you should be walking around after dark." God, he was bad at this. Not only was he making it sound like Victoria might actually be in trouble, but Claire had *just* walked home in the dark, and would have done so alone if Reginald hadn't showed up.

Claire was ignoring him, already pulling on her coat. It was the same coat she'd been wearing when he'd first met her, with the giant anorak hood. It didn't seem nearly as oversized on her anymore.

Reginald squatted down. "I'll make this simple. Either I go alone or we'll sit back down and watch TV. You are flat-out not going with me. Are we clear?"

Claire apparently wasn't used to receiving parental orders. Until recently, Victoria had been a perpetual no-show thanks to her jobs combined with Altus's influence, so Claire was used to doing pretty much what she wanted, when she wanted. Reginald's ultimatum seemed to shock her. Her face registered something that was almost hurt, but then she took the coat off and hung it back up.

"Stay inside," said Reginald.

Then, after he was halfway out the door, he turned and looked Claire in the eye and added, "And not that there's anything to worry about... but be sure to lock the door behind me."

REDNECKS

THE SKY IN CLAIRE'S NEIGHBORHOOD was overcast, and the air was cold. Outside of the cones beneath the streetlights, the night was very dark. All was surprisingly quiet. Reginald sensed a mood of waiting, and of watching.

He walked down the steps to the street, then looked back at the house. Claire looked at him from a window. A woman two houses down was doing the same.

Several ground floor windows on houses along the street were boarded but had lights on upstairs. Either people had moved into boarded houses and not bothered to clear the windows, or citizens were bunking in. Reginald did a quick mental scan of the vampire-related news stories he'd read and seen over the past few weeks, then cross-referenced them with maps from an atlas he'd memorized. As the information clicked, he realized that this neighborhood had seen its share of violence.

He looked back at the boarded windows and was reminded of old-time movie monsters, and the way villagers in those movies would hole up and lay quiet when there was something dark that haunted them during the nights. He got a distinct mental picture that was almost certainly more cinema than reality — humans bunkered and cowering inside of their boarded homes with vampires circling outside, tapping on the windows from dusk until dawn, taunting them, unable to enter.

But it was all fantasy. It was too overt.

For now. But who knows what the next year will bring?

Reginald walked a few minutes down the shady neighborhood street to where Claire had described — a dark throughway that connected two well-lit streets. He was supposed to turn where there was an array of construction pylons and a sign advertising OPEN SEWER. In the middle of the construction barricades was a hole in the concrete with jagged edges. A hole yawned beyond it, leading into a deep and bottomless darkness. It looked like the street had either caved in or been crushed. He found himself wondering how carefully you had to secure a site like this. Would neighborhood kids try to climb down into a dark, smelly sewer?

Reginald turned to look into the alley. It was a straight shot, and the sign on the store from which Victoria was apparently coming was visible from where Reginald was standing. The pass-through was wide but still technically an alley; the backs of buildings bordered it on both sides. Reginald could see dumpsters and discarded shipping palettes.

His vampire eyes could read the writing on stacked boxes, as far away as they were, even in the dark.

Fresh Haas avocados, producto de Honduras.

Hand-Serv Styrofoam cups, 20oz.

And there was something moving off to one side, behind a mound of trash.

Reginald realized that he shouldn't be out searching alone. What if he *did* run into hostile vampires? What the hell was he supposed to do? He wouldn't stand a chance.

His hand stole into his pants pocket, flicking at the edges of a stack of credit cards. He wondered if the office of the Deacon would hold any sway. He had an official card identifying him as the Deacon's deputy, but it was a pathetic thing, no more impressive than a library card. What was he supposed to do, flash it like a badge?

He began walking down the street. He didn't have the speed or stealth of normal vampires, so there was no point in trying to run. If the movement by the trash *was* a vampire (or vampires), his best bet was to approach slowly and hope that their vampire ears wouldn't hear him — not an easy feat for a man who weighed in at three hundred and fifty pounds.

He crept closer, staying to the opposite side of the alley, watching where he stepped, stopping every time he saw movement.

There was definitely someone over there, crouched down. Two someones. They were hunched over something. Could be a discarded pizza box. Could be a crack pipe.

Could be Claire's mother.

Reginald walked closer and realized that it was a pair of homeless people gnawing on a chicken leg. He could see them in the sparse, reflected light from the lit streets on either end of the wide alley. The chicken leg was a sloppy, disgusting thing, slathered in barbecue sauce.

Except that it wasn't barbecue sauce, and it wasn't a chicken leg. It was way too big to be a chicken leg. It had a head on one end. Sticking out of the tiny huddle was a pair sensible shoes. The legs attached to the shoes looked as if they'd been well-toned, perhaps by jogging.

Reginald crouched down. The pair of vampires looked almost feral, the way they were hovered over the woman in the corner. He wondered if she was dead. Most vampires took their prey by force, but Reginald, who glamoured his prey or fed on willing victims, had never witnessed a live, resisting attack. When did they stop fighting? How long did it usually take before they died?

As Reginald watched, one of the legs twitched.

Reginald was still fifteen yards away. There was absolutely no way he'd be able to take the others in a fight. He was slow and weak, and as he'd told Claire, his sole physical talent — superior muscular coordination and balance — was thus far only good for parlor tricks.

Beside him, a splintered shipping palette lay against the alley wall. One of the crossbeams was splintered entirely through. It would make a perfect stake, but it was still stapled to the member underneath it.

Reginald felt his breathing quicken and his heart rate increase. He wished, not for the first time, that movies had gotten vampirism right — that being undead stilled the heart and made the afflicted into perfect undead automatons. But movies hadn't gotten it right. Reginald was fat, he was out of shape, and he was scared.

You'll only get yourself killed, he thought, *and how will that help anyone?*

It was a legitimate question. Reginald was Maurice's greatest weapon thanks to his unparalleled strategic mind. If he died, it would be like unplugging Maurice's master database, leaving him to fly blind into destruction. If he died, there would be nothing standing between the disintegrating Vampire Council and total anarchy.

Reginald pushed the thought down into his shoes. He had to do something. Live or die, there was no way he could simply walk away.

He reached toward the makeshift wooden stake with its protruding staple. He could wiggle the stake until the staple came free, but he'd never be able to do it quietly. So he grabbed the giant staple between his forefinger and thumb and gave a small prayer that what he thought might be true — for a fat guy who could balance on a fencepost and do a one-armed handstand — would end up being true.

He pulled the staple out in one long, slow pull. It came easily, and blessedly quietly.

So it's not just finger coordination, *but an odd level of finger* strength, he thought. *That could come in handy.* Then he almost laughed as he looked at the huddled vampires and thought, *Maybe I can pinch them to death. Or tickle them horribly.*

Reginald gripped the stake in his right hand. It was a pathetic weapon. They'd circle him five times before he could use it.

(Pretend you're a human.)

The thought hit him like a brick. Yes. Of course. If they thought he was a human, they'd attack him in the way they'd attack a human rather than the way they'd attack a vampire. That might just give him enough time to defend himself.

Reginald tucked the stake into the back of his waistband, stepped into the center of the alley, and yelled, "Hey! What are you doing over there?"

Two heads turned, but neither of the vampires bothered to rise to their feet. One was male and one was female. A crazy, random thought crossed Reginald's mind as they assessed him with their fangs out, their mouths smeared with blood: *They're not a couple, because if they were, the woman wouldn't let the man feed on a woman.*

He looked down at the woman in question. It was Victoria. Her eyes were open and vacant. She looked very pale. While he watched, she blinked.

The male vampire hissed, then stood.

Reginald feigned terror. He wasn't a good actor, but he was feeling a decent amount of genuine terror, so he used it. Then he waited, watching their eyes. There was maybe an even chance that they'd recognize him. Reginald was fairly well-known in the vampire community, and the Council's case against him — and the ensuing overthrow — was legendary. But vampires could be like humans in their selective ignorance, and half or more of the country's humans wouldn't recognize the vice president of the United States if he walked up and shook their hand.

The male vampire's eyes met Reginald's. He felt something like an invisible hand touch the top of his head. The vampire was trying to glamour him.

"You are not afraid," the vampire said.

Reginald let his eyes glaze and allowed his shoulders to slump. He assumed the vacant gaze he'd seen so many times through his own eyes.

"Come over here," said the vampire.

Behind the male, the female was getting to her feet. Reginald waited. If he was going to strike, they'd both have to be close — and even then, he doubted he could take both of them. Even if he could stake the male, he'd never move fast enough to get the woman too. She'd either kill him or run. The latter of the two was all he could hope for.

Reginald's hand stole up into the small of his back, slowly, his fingers wrapping around the stake.

The male vampire got closer. Reginald inclined his head slightly, exposing his neck. Soon, the vampire would realize he couldn't smell a human scent on Reginald, but for now the reek of Victoria's blood would mask it. He took a quick glance at her and saw her swallow. She was alive, but couldn't have long. The blood was everywhere.

Reginald freed the stake from his waistband. The woman was still too far away. He took a shambling step forward, inclining his head farther. The woman hissed, her fanged mouth coming open. It was a sound filled with lust and hunger.

In front of Reginald, the male vampire opened his mouth and began to lean forward. Then there was a loud noise and the side of the vampire's head exploded.

Reginald turned in the direction of the sound to see a group of seven or eight humans running down the alley. The man in the lead was holding a handgun at arm's length.

"Fuck you, monster!" he shouted.

The man next to the shooter hooted and fired a second handgun. The shot took the female in the shoulder. A flower of blood bloomed on the wall behind her. The man fired twice more. Since he was only holding on with one hand and was running, both shots went wide. Then the man stopped, sighted, and carefully fired a fourth shot, which hit the female vampire in the eye.

Two of the men in the approaching posse were holding shotguns, but they hadn't so much as raised them. There seemed to be an order to the attack that they all understood, as if they'd done this before. The shotguns, with their wide radius, were probably intended for close-quarters work. They probably only came up after the lead men had winged their quarry with the smaller guns. Reginald couldn't help calculating as he watched them run. He was thinking that they could step up their game by investing in a rifle or two.

The male vampire stood up. The side of his previously coifed hairdo was matted with blood. He touched it in revulsion. He then bent down to check on the female, but choosing to duck rather than attack was a mistake. The moment's hesitation gave the men enough time to sight and fire again. Three bullets smashed into the male's chest, throwing him backward into the wall and seducing a groan. Then the shotgun-bearers finally got into the action as the group arrived around Reginald. They trained their barrels on the female and opened fire, blowing a C-shaped hole in her side.

The male was already halfway healed. He hissed, but Reginald, who the posse was ignoring, could hear the pain in that hiss. Gunshots wouldn't stop a vampire unless they were silver or wood and struck him in the heart, but they hurt like hell and could definitely slow one down.

The group of men (Reginald counted eight now that they'd formed a firing line and were standing still) fired shot after shot into the pair of vampires, backing them away from Victoria. One of the men shouted to watch out for a victim on the ground. Blood was absolutely everywhere. The vampires refused to stay down. They healed quickly, but every time they got to their feet, the men with the guns fired again and knocked them back down.

The female, finding herself temporarily unshot, crouched, jumped, and landed on the three-story roof of the building behind her. Reginald looked up, but she was already gone in a blur.

The male vampire was struggling to get his feet. Literally. The barrage of bullets had torn off one of his feet. Reginald watched as the foot turned to ash inside of his shoe and a new one, shoeless, grew at the end of his ragged leg. Watching the male try to get up was like watching a person struggle forward into the stream from a pressure hose. But it was just a standoff; the vampire couldn't heal fast enough to flee, and the group would never kill him with normal metal slugs.

The vampire, barely recognizable for all the blood, gripped a ladder hanging from the building's roof and began to climb — slowly, because all of his energy seemed to be going into healing. Then the shotgunners, both of whom had been reloading, raised their weapons, took several steps forward now that the creature was retreating, and fired, and fired, and fired until they were empty. When the smoke cleared, the vampire was hanging from the ladder by his hands. His torso was hanging on by a small band of something — maybe skin, maybe tendon, maybe even intestine. Reginald could see that his spine had already been snapped. It was sticking out at a strange angle.

Then the tendon or whatever it was gave way, and the vampire's lower half fell to the ground with a *Fwump*. The legs immediately turned gray under the vampire's now-discarded pants and began to flake away. The top half of the vampire continued to clamber up the ladder hand-over-hand, screaming in pain. Then a bulbous pink balloon began to grow where he'd been halved. The balloon elongated, and by the time the vampire reached the top rung, the pink had become peach and had formed the beginnings of new legs and a naked ass.

The men appeared too shocked to speak or to continue firing after the escaping half of a vampire. The shotgunners were empty and hadn't bothered to reload. They all watched as the vampire reached the roof and vanished.

One of the men stooped toward Victoria, who was hard to find amongst all of the blood. Where had all of the blood come from? Reginald had never gotten a satisfactory answer to that. Vampires could bleed and bleed and bleed, and they'd never run out.

"You okay, mister?" said one of the men, looking over at Reginald. "He didn't get you before we showed up, did he?"

Reginald nodded at the first question, then shook his head at the second. He bared his neck to show the man.

"Those things just keep coming," said one of the men holding a shotgun. "We've found that all we can do is to drive them back."

"They're *vampires*," said a boy at the back of the group, who was holding only a bat. Whether he'd had a gun drawn at any point, Reginald hadn't seen.

"Shut up, Greg," said the man who'd led the charge.

"He saw what just happened," said Greg. "You saw it, right? We ain't crazy."

Reginald shrugged, unsure how to get out of this situation. He didn't want to stick around and face the police — if, in fact, the police showed up. But they'd have to. The noise of the encounter had been thunderous. Dozens of shots had been fired. Every house for miles must have called 911.

"Can you stick around for an ambulance if we call one?" said the man who'd asked if he was okay. "There'll be a lot of questions for eight guys with weapons standing over a woman covered in ten gallons of blood. We've gotta go. You tell them whatever you want, okay?"

Reginald nodded.

"Listen... I know you're scared, but... what's your name, buddy?"

"Floyd," said Reginald. But he *was* scared, and there was a lot of blood, and apparently his body enjoyed coming up with new and amusing ways to betray him. So, when he opened his mouth, the neighborly expression dropped off of the man's face and he began fumbling with the safety on his handgun.

"He's got fangs!" the man yelled.

In the seconds it took for the other men to turn and raise their guns, Reginald threw his weight into a tall stack of palettes and ran. The stack wobbled and fell behind him, striking two of the men in the lead and creating an obstacle for the rest.

The reach of their guns was unimpaired by the palettes, however.

The first gunman fired and hit Reginald in the back. It must not have hit any bones, because Reginald watched a red bloom form on the front of his shirt as the bullet passed straight through him. They were going to try and bring him down like they'd done the others, so he'd have to grit his teeth through the pain and force his legs to keep working. If he fell, he was done for. The man called Greg had said they were vampires. Sooner or later, one of the men would think to break off a piece of wood and stick it into the fat guy to see what happened. In fact, said fat guy had made it easy.

He had a stake tucked into the waistband of his pants.

The bullet wound felt like someone had shoved a very hot spike through Reginald's side. He felt himself wanting to favor that side, but he made his arms keep pumping, driving him forward.

The first of the men were over the fallen palettes, now thirty yards back. The shotgunners, thankfully, were at the very rear of the group. It would take them time to reload, and it wasn't easy to do so while running.

The pain of the gunshot passed, but Reginald was already feeling lightheaded and damning his vampire inabilities. He could sprint over short distances, and he'd found that if he did, he could outrun humans for a minute or two... but once the sprint gave out, even moderately fit humans easily overtook him.

There was no question they'd catch up. He couldn't lead them to Claire's house even if he could get there, which he couldn't. He didn't know where to go. But he'd need to find a way out in the next sixty seconds, or it would all be over.

Two more shots struck him. The first hit him in the hip, causing fantastic pain to race down his leg. The second ripped the side of his head open. There was a moment of confusion while his brain healed, then a red cloud of agony. Healing took a good ten seconds, and the ripping sensation down his leg and in the back of his head made those seconds intolerable. He started to stagger. To weave. He felt the pain threatening to kick his legs out from under him, and then it would all be over.

But then, time stopped.

It didn't really stop, of course, but Reginald suddenly found himself with the same slow-motion clarity he'd experienced while reading for the first time as a vampire. Back in his living room, with Maurice watching, he remembered how seconds had dilated into hours. He'd read an entire book at what felt like a normal speed, then had come out of his trance to find that the second hand of the clock had only advanced a few clicks.

Reginald's awareness took in the scene around him. The men were behind him, frozen. He still hurt, but he was no longer staggering. Nothing was happening. Nothing at all.

Am I becoming fast? Am I becoming strong?

But no, that wasn't it. His brain was simply processing quickly. *Super* quickly. So quickly that events outside of his mind seemed to take no time at all by comparison. He'd probably always been able to do this, but had just now realized it. It was as if he'd unlocked a new achievement in the game of vampirism. He'd leveled up.

Could he move faster? Could he use this span of this timelessness to elude them?

Reginald tried to move his arms and his legs, but they were trapped in slow, cold tar.

So it's just my mind that's fast.

And that made sense, but it didn't help him any. Sure, he could assess his situation all he wanted, but assessing didn't change his predicament. There were still eight men behind him with guns, and his body still couldn't move fast enough or for long enough to elude them. He had two choices: he could wait here forever, trapped in a frozen moment in time, or he could wind the reel forward and watch himself die in agonizing detail.

Reginald sensed his body.

His exhaustion was distant and far-off. He was aware that his muscles and lungs would only last for so much longer in real time, but none of that mattered. You couldn't draw breath in the space of a thought, and whatever mind-presence he was in now didn't need to breathe. But the pain. The *pain* was real. Even now, even in timelessness, the pain was making it hard to think. The pain was the problem. He could deal with exhaustion, but the *pain* slowed him down even more. The *pain* was allowing his pursuers to close the gap. The *pain* was causing him to stagger and weave. The *pain* was about to make him trip.

The pain will bring you down, so you have to turn it off, said a voice.

It wasn't Reginald's voice. It was as if he were hearing it on a loudspeaker, in his head, in an anteroom of frozen time. Where had he heard that voice before?

Turn off the pain, the voice repeated, *so that you'll have a chance.*

Turn it off? he thought.

Turn it off, said the voice.

The idea didn't make sense.

But then, quite suddenly, he saw how to do it. It was as if he'd been in a dark room and someone had turned on a light. He saw where the pain came from and where it went, and he saw how to break the circuit. He flipped a switch inside of himself. The knife slicing down the length of his leg vanished. The ache in his head vanished.

Now go, said the voice.

Time resumed without warning.

The mental controls slipped and skittered under Reginald's metaphorical hands as the voice pushed him rudely back into the world against his will. It was as if Reginald, even with his hands on the wheel of his mind, hadn't been able to avoid a patch of black ice. He found himself barreling forward again in the dark alley, the men behind him.

But the pain was gone. Totally gone. He felt fine. He was short of breath, and in a moment, his legs would give out from exhaustion. But there was no pain.

There were two more shots behind him. Both struck him just below the shoulder blades. Their impact felt like a heavy tap on the back, nothing more.

He felt himself pass the patch of mental black ice and felt his control return. What he'd just done, he knew he could do again. He took a quick glance around to give himself a visual map, then went into his mind and felt everything grind to a stop like a dying clock. The world froze around him. And he thought.

I can't go forward.

I can't go backward.

I can't go up. Even if a pipe would support me, they'd cut me in half before I reached a roof.

But there was nothing left. There was nowhere else to go.

But then he thought: *Go down.*

And in the still moment inside of his mind, Reginald looked forward and saw the jagged hole in the street. Into the sewer.

Two voices began to bicker inside of him.

Who knows what's down there?

It doesn't matter, considering what's up here.

I don't know where it leads.

You do *know where your current course leads, and it's nowhere good.*

I'll never fit.

You have to.

And he *did* have to. Claire's mother had just been attacked, maybe killed, and Victoria was all Claire had. Maurice depended on him for his strategy, and the strategic direction Maurice took could decide the fates of thousands — both human and vampire. The war had already started. The evidence was right behind him, splattered all over the wall in the alley.

Reginald allowed time to resume.☐

He could see the construction pylons thirty yards ahead. The men behind him were gaining, still firing. He was almost out of energy, but he *had* to make it. His legs slowed. He forced them to keep moving, knowing that normally they'd feel intensely painful, as if they were on fire. His chest wanted to seize, but he pushed through it.

Another bullet struck him in the back of the neck. It didn't hurt, but it knocked him down. Down to the ground.

Get up.

I can't.

Get up!

I can't!

And he couldn't. As he healed, as the men gained on him, the slug fell through his neck and onto the concrete with a noise like a dropped quarter. He couldn't get his breath. It wasn't a matter of will. It wasn't a matter of fighting through the pain, because there was no pain. It was a matter of his inability to function. Too much lactic acid, paralyzing his muscles so that they could recover. You couldn't fight biology, even if you were a vampire.

GET UP, YOU FAT MOTHERFUCKER, AND RUN!

The men hadn't slowed. They were getting very close — into shotgun range, anyway.

As Reginald stumbled onto his feet and made his final approach to the pylons, a blast from the rear struck him full in the back and he pitched forward, into one of the large orange and white cones. For what felt like the dozenth time since he'd become a vampire, Reginald felt his nose break.

They were twenty yards back.

Ten.

He had his arms inside of the hole, his vampire eyes barely making out a shallow stream of disgusting water at the bottom, fifteen or twenty feet down. He was going in head-first. If he made it, this was going to be unpleasant. But that was irrelevant, because he *wasn't* going to make it.

He was stuck.

Feeling more bullets strike his lower half (many in his ass; what the hell), Reginald hung above the sewer with his head, arms, and shoulders dangling like a man trapped in a snare, his gut wedged firmly in the hole in the concrete.

The posse of men arrived above him. Reginald knew they'd arrived because he could hear them and because the number of bullets and buckshot striking him increased. He was very, very thankful he wasn't experiencing pain, because the pain in this moment had to be a whopper.

"What the fuck! He's wedged into that hole!" yelled one of the men.

"Should we pull him out?" said another.

"Don't get close!"

"How could this guy be a monster? I mean, look at him."

106

More gunshots. In a distant, pain-free way, it felt like one of his feet might almost be severed. The men would be able to start a whole collection of vampire shoes.

"Pull him out!" said one of the earlier voices. Reginald thought it might be Greg, the guy who believed in vampires.

"Why?"

"You want him to get away?"

Hands grabbed Reginald's legs. His foot seemed to have regrown, because he felt someone tugging at both of them. This went on for a few minutes, and then the hands let go.

"Jesus," said a voice. "He's really wedged in there."

Reginald hung in the blackness, wondering if there was a limit to the humiliation a person could endure before he snapped.

"Man, he's a fat fucker," said a voice.

From inside of the hole, Reginald yelled, "Get off my back. It's glandular."

A foot pressed on his ass, then began to stomp in earnest.

A voice said, "What the hell are you doing?"

"Figured I'd try to push him through."

"You dumbass. He'll get away."

"What? They can't be killed, except... Oh!"

Reginald waited to see what the voice had just realized, then felt something poking him randomly around the midsection, where he was wedged in the hole.

"Damn," the voice said. "He's too far in."

"What were you going to do?"

"I figured I could pound a stake through his heart."

"Oh."

Minutes passed. Reginald hung upside-down in the darkness, his arms over his head and swinging. "So, you guys from around here?" said Reginald.

"We should just leave him," said one of the men.

The stake continued to poke him, trying to find a way in.

"Knock it off, Teddy."

The stake kept probing. "I thought I might be able to angle it in through his stomach. But I think there's too much fat in the way."

"It used to be hard for me to give blood for the same reason," Reginald said conversationally. It occurred to him that it stunk in here. And why not? It was a sewer.

The men were silent for a few moments. Finally someone said, "Well, what should we do?"

Reginald said, "Let's play twenty questions."

There was another brief moment, and then one of the men said, "What time is it?"

"They have to be 'yes' or 'no' questions," said Reginald.

"Maybe a few minutes past eleven?" said the first man, ignoring him.

"We'll just have to wait until sunrise," said the second.

"No," said Reginald. "You now have nineteen questions remaining."

"That's all damn night!" said the man who'd reported the time. "What are we supposed to do, get lawn chairs and camp out?"

"Yes," said Reginald. "Eighteen left."

There was a gunshot, and Reginald felt a bullet explode into his right buttcheek.

"We can't just stay here all night. The cops will be here any minute." He paused, as if something was occurring to him. "Shit. You've already called 911."

The other man sighed. "All right, fine. We'll go. I don't think he's going anywhere. The sun can finish him off."

Reginald thought, *Shit. The sun.*

"Hey!" he yelled. "Which one of you lives three blocks away and has the ugly wife who won't shut up?"

Two or three distinct voices made disturbed murmurs. One voice was louder than the others. Reginald addressed it.

"I fucked your wife, buddy," he said. In truth, he had no idea who the men were, who their wives or families were, or where they'd come from. But they'd arrived on foot and looked like rednecks. The chances of one of them living a few blocks away and considering his wife an ugly nag seemed pretty good.

One or two of the voices murmured. A third shrieked, "You stay away from my ugly wife!"

"I fucked her earlier, and as soon as you leave, I'm going to use my monster powers to get out of here and warp over there and eat her brains while fucking her again."

"Which one of us are you talking to?" said one of the others.

"All three of you. I fucked them all. There's the ugly woman in the shitty house, the ugly woman in the house with the shitty car in the driveway, and the ugly woman with the Ted Nugent tattoo." The last was a long shot, but Reginald almost laughed when one of the men screamed like a girl. But still nobody was reacting, so Reginald thrashed from the waist down, kicking his legs out and twitching.

"What's he doing?" yelled the man who'd spoken earlier. There was a note of panic in his voice.

"I'm preparing my monster warp. *Muhahaha!*"

"Stop him, Greg!"

"In a minute I'll vanish, and then I can't wait to visit each of your ugly wives and cut their heads open and play with their brains while I fuck them in the eye sockets and..."

The composition of the men broke and they all began firing their guns at point-blank range. As they did, large chunks of Reginald began to peel off and fly away. Reginald could feel it happening. It was distant without the pain, and almost interesting. He could sense parts of his body until they were severed, and then he lost their awareness. He felt shotgun blasts blowing holes in his back, his legs, and the exposed part of his overhanging belly.

"Afterward," Reginald screamed over the gunshots, "I'm going to head over and fuck your ugly *mothers*!"

The guns fired faster.

Finally, enough of Reginald's stomach had been eroded away that he — more or less just his upper half, now — fell head-first down the hole. He plummeted to the hole's concrete bottom and found himself in feculent, smelly water. He tried to stand up, but what remained below his belt was like a giant pink tadpole's tail.

Except that he *had* no belt. And what was somehow worse, no lower half meant no pants.

Something fell from above. It looked like a sack full of meat, but when it hit the bottom, it exploded in a grey cloud, lit from the dim streetlight above. It was what used to be his legs, and was now just his pants. They were shredded beyond belief, but once he'd totally healed, he stood up and pulled them on. Incredible Hulk pants were better than no pants any day of the week.

Reginald looked up. The heads of eight men in a circle stared down at him, not one of them angry or bold. All of the men looked absolutely terrified.

"Hey!" Reginald yelled. "Whose girlfriend has the bedazzled shirt that says, 'Mega Cum Slut'?"

"Mine!" yelled one of the heads.

"Jesus, really?" said Reginald.

"What about her?"

"I'm going there now." He gave a dramatic moan and waved his arms. "Run, run!"

The heads vanished. Reginald heard feet running away, and then he began the long slog in the dark toward wherever the sewer led him.

HULK

REGINALD KNOCKED ON NIKKI'S DOOR about an hour before sunrise. She opened the door to find him covered in blood, smelling like sewer, his shirt in shreds and his pants not much more substantial than a grass skirt. His hair was packed with dirt and gore and had wedged up into a fauxhawk before hardening.

He crossed the room, slapped an assortment of shiny metal balls into Nikki's palm, and began to undress on a threadbare area rug. Once he was done, he balled the rug up and put it near the trashcan, then sat nude on the couch.

Nikki stared at him.

"I don't want to talk about it," he said.

But they did, briefly, with Reginald simply trying to keep up with his own memories as he spoke. He was exhausted. At some point — possibly in the middle of a sentence — he fell asleep.

An indeterminate amount of time later, Reginald awoke to find that he'd been rubbed somewhat cleaner and dressed in pajamas. The clock on the wall indicated that the sun must be up, but Nikki was awake, a cordless phone in her hand.

"She's fine," said Nikki, raising the phone.

"Who's fine?"

"Claire's mother. You told me to call around?"

Reginald sat up. He felt hung over. He rubbed his head, feeling as if he'd overtaxed it. All of last night was there inside of his mind, but it was foggy, and it hurt to think. His mouth felt dry. There was an empty Cheetos bag in front of him. He remembered annihilating the Cheetos before sleep took him, and of showing them no mercy.

"Oh, right." He put both hands on his forehead.

Nikki walked to the couch and sat next to him. She tried to run a hand through his hair. It was hard and stiff, so she ran her hand over the top of it instead, like rubbing a turtle's shell.

"Some weird stuff happened last night," said Reginald.

"You said you stopped time."

"Not literally. But that's what it felt like."

Nikki punched him in the side of the head.

"Ow, hell!" he yelled.

"Sorry. I wanted to see if you were still impervious to pain. Apparently you're not. But last night, you kept telling me to kick you in the balls, and you just kept laughing all the while. Do you remember?"

"Yes." It had seemed hilarious at the time, but he'd been in no condition to judge hilarity when he'd come home. He'd been half dead, which was saying something for a person who was already mostly dead even when fully functional.

114

Nikki seemed unsure what to say next, so she again held up the phone. "Anyway, she's at Mercy. Apparently an ambulance showed up and found her where your buddies described. They're saying she was stabbed."

"Stabbed?"

Nikki nodded. "Then, I told them I was Victoria's sister and asked what they were doing for her. The man I talked to didn't want to tell me, but I cry well on cue. He looked some stuff up and said that they gave her a bunch of blood and stitched up her wounds, and that she should be fine. But from what he said, it's good that you showed up when you did. Those vampires weren't going to sip and ship. They were going to drink until she was dry."

"It wasn't me. Thank that gang of rednecks."

Nikki snorted.

"And you talked to Claire?"

Nikki pursed her lips. Reginald sat up. "What?"

"She was there. I guess they're going to let her sleep there tonight, even. But she wouldn't come to the phone."

"Did she know it was you?"

Nikki nodded. "I told the guy to tell her it was Aunt Nikki and Uncle Reginald. She didn't want to talk."

"Upset," said Reginald. But he wondered if there was more he was forgetting, or more that he was failing to work out.

"Any news on the posse?"

115

"I suppose Claire would have been able to tell me if she heard shots, but the guy I talked to knew nothing, or was disclosing nothing."

Reginald sighed. It was all falling apart. Vampires were openly killing humans. Humans were starting to believe that there were real monsters in the world. The other night, he'd even seen a news report featuring eyewitnesses who said they'd watched several "creatures" flee the site of brutal killings by leaping up onto the tops of buildings and "vanishing in blurs." There was only so much stubborn disbelief to go around.

Reginald stood from the couch and stumbled toward the bathroom. Nikki followed him, asking when he last ate. Reginald told her he'd eaten Cheetos before falling asleep, and Nikki said that wasn't what she meant.

"You need blood," said Nikki.

"Blood is disgusting," said Reginald.

"Let me order a pizza man," said Nikki.

"Make sure it comes with a pizza," said Reginald.

STRESS

AFTER HIS PIZZA MAN AND his pizza, Reginald announced that he was going to take a shower because it was almost time to go to work.

Nikki's jaw dropped. She threw her hands into the air and asked how *going to work* — given all that had happened and was happening — could possibly be on his mind. Reginald asked her how she was planning to pay her rent without working. Nikki said that Maurice would give them both money, because he already had way, way too much. Reginald said that he refused to be a charity case. Nikki said that Reginald could long ago have glamoured his bosses and sat home forever, collecting checks for doing nothing.

Reginald said that he'd once asked Maurice why *he* worked, given that he had a whole immortal, wealthy existence in front of him. Maurice had replied that sometimes, it was nice to be a mindless idiot. Reginald said that at the time, he didn't understand why Maurice would say such a ridiculous thing... but that now, he did.

Nikki had nothing to say to that.

Reginald rose from the couch and walked to the bathroom, then stepped into the shower and let the hot water begin to dissolve the crud in his hair.

He bent his head forward, watching the drain as the water flowed red and brown around his feet. Eventually the water became more or less clear, and he turned his face toward the spray.

Reginald — like his maker — insisted on keeping feet in both the human and vampire worlds. Most would have seen it as a step in the wrong direction, but for Reginald, having a double life functioned as a safety valve. Vampires were usually powerful, strong, and above laws and morality, making vampire life an ideal escape from the drudgery of human existence. For Reginald, however, who had a vampire life filled with inadequacy and disintegration and decay, *human* life was his escape. When things got bad, he sometimes stayed up until all hours of the day, watching talk shows and eating junk food. At those times, he *relished* going to work. He *reveled* in the abuse of his annoying co-workers and bosses. He supposed he was as goth inside as Maurice looked on the outside. He longed for the pain of humanity so that he could feel alive for a while — instead of undead, surrounded by failed responsibility and chaos.

And there was so much chaos lately.

Every night, on the news, there were more and more gruesome murders. The networks had to be loving it. They'd been blessed with a neverending supply of blood-spattered walls and gore-strewn rooms to photograph. The police shooed the news crews away over and over again, but all they had to do was to go down the street, where there was always another gathering, another person dead, another report of carnage and destruction... and, more and more often, another report of inhuman creatures that managed incredible feats.

What made it worse was that everyone Reginald trusted and believed in seemed to be looking to *him* for answers. As if he knew more than they did. As if memory and deduction meant anything now that so many butterfly wings were stirring distant hurricanes. Reginald wanted someone to give *him* the answers, but nobody had answers to give. Instead, they asked. And asked. And asked. And Reginald did his best to help where he could, but so often, he came up empty.

Even the Europeans were no help. He'd spoken to Karl, head of the European Vampire Council, a few times via Skype. News from Luxembourg was that the angel Santos seemed to have finally kicked his earthly addiction and had vanished without a trace. Most of the European and Asian vampires watched the news out of America and were active on Fangbook. Karl didn't want to come right out and say it because he was proud, but as went America, so went the world. He said that the EU Council had held together, but that vigilante gangs were proliferating there as they were in the US. *They're terrified*, Karl told Reginald and Maurice, *and murder is all they know to do well.*

Maurice and Reginald couldn't reason with murderers. Their position was untenable. They wanted the killing and reckless creation to end. And in its place, they wanted the frightened vampire population to do... *what*, exactly? At the Ring of Fire, Balestro had spoken of evolution, but evolution was vague and open to interpretation. Evolution took time. Nobody wanted to analyze and soul-search and wait. They wanted a fix, and they wanted it *now.*

And what was worse, Reginald was beginning to think that maybe he and Maurice were the crazy ones. Maybe what was happening in the world and on the news *was* what the angels wanted. Vampires were the descendants of Cain and the servants of darkness, after all. Was it really that insane to imagine that chaos and murder and rape and death were what the darkness wanted?

The hot water ran over Reginald's skull. He willed it to wash away his worries. It was all too much.

Claire's mother.

Claire's cold shoulder.

Guns and blood and defied orders of protection.

His odd new abilities, which he didn't understand: the way his mind could stop time to think, and his (apparently temporary) ability to turn off pain, right when he needed it most.

Was this what Balestro had given him, that night on the hilltop? And if it was, *why* had Balestro given it to him? Did the fact that Balestro had given him something mean that Balestro wanted Reginald to win the battle that was raging? Was Reginald on the angels' side, or was he against them?

But of all the questions and doubts circling in his mind, what bothered Reginald most of all was a troubling certainty that he might simply be too weak to face what was coming. When Nikki had her epiphany about blood ties and thirst, she had simply stopped feeding more than was strictly necessary. She'd seen what needed to be done and had the will to do it, but Reginald had never developed that kind of will power and fortitude.

How can I promote evolution in the Nation if I can't evolve myself? he'd asked her. And she'd had no answer.

It was too much. Being human had been so much easier.

Reginald dried off, wrapped a towel around his waist, and walked out to get his clothes before remembering that he'd spent the day at Nikki's apartment and had none. So once the sun had set, she ran back to his house and was back in seconds with clean underwear, slacks, a shirt, and shoes. Reginald used Nikki's deodorant and brushed his teeth with his finger. He noticed that his fangs never got brushed, because he never brushed his teeth when he was angry, hungry, or horny. Then he wondered why he brushed his teeth at all. It wasn't like they'd ever decay or fall out. He supposed the ritual comforted him, just like junk food and TV comforted him.

Old habits simply died hard, like so many people did these days.

Reginald walked out of the bathroom to find Nikki standing in the hallway stark naked, a come-hither expression on her face.

"We don't have to leave for a half hour," she said. "And I'd like to prescribe some much-needed stress relief for you."

"I'm a monster," he said vacantly.

"*I* think you're still human," she said, walking toward him and running his shirt collar between her fingers, "but let's check, just to be sure."

BLOODBATH

WHEN THEY ARRIVED AT THE office an hour later, they found the front door ajar. The sight of it made foreboding rise in Reginald's gut.

There was no good reason for foreboding. The day shift would all be gone by now, and Walker and the custodians would be in the building alone unless someone had decided to work late. Any one of the departing day shift workers could have broken the closer on their way out, and nobody in the company would care enough to close the door when it failed to close on its own. In fact, Reginald would have thought things were more out of place if the closer were broken and someone *had* closed the door. Courtesy, in Reginald's workplace, was suspicious in and of itself.

But still, when he noticed the box above the door hanging from its broken mounting, he raised an arm to stop Nikki from going any farther. Something about it bothered him, especially with the hangover from his earlier dark thoughts still swimming in his mind. It reminded him of the door at the top of the Asbury's basement staircase — also ajar, also dangling an arm from a broken pneumatic closer. The door in that club had said so many troubling things. It said that order and security had ceased to matter. It said that entropy had become a stronger force than paranoia — and according to Maurice, paranoia had been the Council's hallmark for centuries. The ajar door at the Asbury had symbolized everything within the Nation that was falling apart.

And now here was another ajar door. It was stupid to back away from it, but he did it anyway.

"The door is open," said Reginald when Nikki gave him a questioning look.

"Yeah?"

"It reminds me of the door at the Council."

Nikki pushed his hand down gently. The small gesture said that she understood, but that Reginald had been on edge lately and might not be the best judge of what was worth fretting about.

"Many doors are similar," she said.

Reginald felt a breeze at his back. A second later, Maurice appeared on his other side.

"Are we having a standoff?" he said.

"You came to work!" said Nikki. Maurice hadn't been bothering with work lately, but he looked as haggard as Reginald felt. Apparently, they felt the same way about the redeeming powers of bureaucracy and pointless paperwork.

"I needed monotony," said Maurice. "I wanted to spend some time doing something that has utterly no meaning whatsoever. I needed to be somewhere where if I make a huge error, nobody even notices."

"Something is wrong," said Reginald, eyeing the door.

He hadn't put Nikki's keys into his pocket. She had a tiny Swiss Army knife on the chain — not a very ladylike accessory, he'd always thought. Reginald was holding it as if he planned to open it and do battle. The entire knife was two inches long. Whatever threat he sensed was in for a serious miniature nail-filing.

"See you inside," said Maurice, slapping Reginald on the back and walking forward. "I feel like having a cup of coffee out of a mug that expresses my dislike for Mondays."

Nikki rubbed the back of Reginald's neck and looked into his eyes. "Come on," she said.

Reginald ignored her, still staring at the office door across the parking lot.

"Maurice," he said.

Maurice turned, then gave a tiny start as his eyes flicked down.

Reginald had opened the blade of the knife and had driven it through the palm of his hand. Blood ran down his pinky finger and pattered onto the concrete.

"I can't feel it," said Reginald.

"What do you mean, *you can't feel it?*" said Maurice.

"Something new. I'll explain later," said Reginald. "For now, take my word for it that something is wrong here." He pulled the knife from his palm, stooped to wipe the blade on the grass at the back of his parking spot, and closed it. He pocketed the keys, then began walking slowly toward the door.

They walked into the lobby with Reginald in the lead. There was a second door in front of them that led into the office and an elevator to the right. The elevator was supposed to be for handicapped use, but before becoming a vampire, Reginald had used to use it when he needed to go upstairs. On the doors of the elevator, handwritten in large red letters, were the words ONLY HUMAN.

Maurice leaned forward. Nikki told him not to touch it, but Maurice was only sniffing.

"Blood," he said.

But of course it was blood, and of course the message wasn't for just anyone, but for Maurice specifically. Anti-establishment propaganda over the past few months had been dominated by one key phrase where violence against non-vampires was concerned: *They're only human.* It had become the slogan of Maurice's political opposition, who tried to paint Maurice as a leader willing to sacrifice vampire welfare in favor of human welfare. Maurice was willing to destroy them all, they said. And for what? Those he sided with weren't immortal. They weren't strong. They weren't worthy. They didn't need or deserve protection. They were, in the end, *only human.*

Maurice's mouth was open. His fangs were out.

"Try not to touch anything," said Reginald, but Maurice was already gone. The inner door fluttered closed behind him.

Reginald looked at Nikki and saw that her fangs were out as well. On Nikki, fangs looked both sexy and dangerous. On Reginald, fangs looked pathetic. Unglamoured humans paled when they saw Nikki, but laughed when they saw Reginald.

They pushed into the office to find it covered in blood.

Reginald walked through the aisles between the cubicles slowly, trying to make sense of what he saw. Nikki split off, exploring in gape-mouthed awe. The lights were all on, instead of the smaller set that was usually lit after the day shift left. In the brightness, they could see everything there was to see. Everyone was dead. The entire day shift.

Scott, who was mocked because he was old.

Noel, who was mocked because she was plain.

Along with several of the homogenous males who'd mocked them, all of their bodies severed into sections and thrown haphazardly about — everyone finally equal at the moment of their murder.

In the office at the end of the hall, Reginald found Berger. At the other end, he found several of the frat boy types who looked just like Walker, all with their perfect white teeth stained crimson.

He caught up with Maurice in the break room where, on the break room table, they found five coffee cups. All of the cups were stained and half-filled with blood. Maurice leaned down and sniffed at one of them.

"So much blood that they couldn't drink it all," he said. Then he kicked one of the small chairs across the room, where it shattered a full pitcher of orange juice that had been sitting on the counter. Yellow liquid ran onto the floor and mingled with bloody footprints, creating a deep orange. Then Maurice pointed at the table and the mugs as if Reginald and Nikki were to blame. "They bled them into mugs, and they sat here and drank it," he spat. "Look at the mugs. Mine. Yours, Reginald. Nikki's. This is my backup mug. This one I don't know."

The cup said THICK DICK.

"It's Walker's," said Reginald.

"They did it for us. They set this up for us, directed at us, as a message to me, their powerless leader. They opened people up, they collected their blood, and then they sat here and they laughed. I saw several people out there, missing parts of their bodies, dead at the end of long streaks of gore. They dragged themselves down hallways, trying to get away. The bastards didn't even glamour them."

Nikki was starting to cry. It was a strange thing for a vampire to do over death and blood, Reginald thought, but he put his arm around her nonetheless. He felt it too. He didn't like many of these people, but they'd had friends and families, and they'd been alive just a few hours earlier, blissfully unaware of what was awaiting them.

"This is so stupid," said Nikki, her voice hitching. "We've shed our share of blood."

"Not like this," said Reginald.

"We have to do something," she said.

"What can we do?" said Maurice. "There's no crime here. They're... they were... *only human*, after all."

Nikki shook her head. There was no way out. The only authorities who would care were human authorities, and the human authorities hadn't figured out what they were up against. And even if they did figure it out, what power would they have against vampires? Were Reginald, Nikki, and Maurice supposed to ally with humans against their own kind? Were they supposed to turn traitors? And if they did, what would come of the vampires they counted as friends?

"We can't do a goddamn thing," said Maurice. "We just have to... to *take* it."

But even beyond Maurice and Nikki's senses of desperation, Reginald felt uneasy. There was more here than what they'd seen so far. He'd known that something was wrong outside, when what he was starting to think of as his Spidey Sense — call it "Reginald Sense" — had started to tingle. But even now, with all of the bloody cards on the table, that new sense was still tingling. His mind still felt hyper-aware. If he were to open the knife and stick himself with it, he was sure he still wouldn't feel it. There was more here to find. Something else unpleasant to unearth.

"Why is Walker's coffee cup on the table with ours?" he said.

Maurice shrugged.

Reginald made a slow, pacing circuit of the table. He stepped over the spilled orange juice on the far side, then came around to his own coffee cup. He lowered his head to the cup, paused when the lip was just under his nose, and inhaled deeply.

Then he straightened up, took a few steps forward, leaned toward Maurice's main coffee cup, and did the same. He repeated the action for Nikki's cup and Maurice's backup.

Finally, he stood over Walker's cup, bent, and inhaled deeply.

"A human used this cup," he said.

He stood and walked up in front of Maurice.

"Did you find Walker out there?"

"No," said Maurice.

"Find him," said Reginald.

They spread out into the office and began to open closets, look under desks, and pound on doors. It was Maurice who eventually found him. Walker was in the coat closet at the end of the hall, his entire front covered in blood. His tie was askew, his hair a matted mess. It looked like he'd crawled through a river of blood, or had laid down in one. He was very much alive, his eyes terrified, his face wet with tears and snot.

Maurice called to Reginald and Nikki. They came over and stood in front of the closet, and all three of them watched Walker snivel and panic. It was hard to believe that this pathetic shell had once tormented all of them.

"Walker," said Reginald. "What happened here?"

But Walker said nothing. He just shivered and hugged his legs to his chest and continued to stare up as if he'd been beaten.

Reginald squatted in front of him. A few months back, a squat would have thrown him over onto his back, but now he easily balanced on the tops of his toes, his forearms resting on his knees.

"Did you see who did this?" he asked.

"Everyone is dead," said Walker.

"Yes."

"I called 911. I called it when I heard them coming back." There was a cell phone on the floor, its case caked with blood from Walker's filthy hands. Reginald picked it up and looked through the call history. He'd called 911 just a few minutes ago, when they themselves had come in.

"What did you tell them?"

"There's so much blood," said Walker. "It's everywhere. I didn't know what to do. I'm sorry. I'm sorry." Fluid was dripping from his nose. His face was working, his handsome features becoming ugly and alien.

"It's not your fault," said Reginald.

Walker looked up, his eyes firmly on Reginald's. Reginald's new sense tingled. There was something strange in Walker's eyes —

something he'd never seen before. Fear. Helplessness. Panic.

"Tell me who did this," said Reginald.

"It's all my fault. The blood, Reggie. It was like someone was throwing water balloons, the way it flew. And there was so much screaming. It's all my fault."

"How many were there?" said Reginald.

"Four."

"How did you escape? How did you get away from them?"

"It's all my fault, Reggie," said Walker. His eyes were wet, pleading. "All of these people. They're all... gone." It looked like he was trying to swallow but couldn't manage. His throat worked and hitched, his perfect adam's apple bobbing up and down. His upper lip quivered. It almost looked like he had a lump of something under it along the top, as if the vampires had surprised him while he was having a good chew and spit.

"Walker," said Reginald. "Tell me what they looked like."

"It's my fault they're dead, Reggie," said Walker, his eyes pleading.

Maurice nudged Reginald with his foot. Reginald looked up. Maurice tapped his upper lip just below his right nostril. Right where Walker had his lump of chewing tobacco.

"Walker," said Reginald. "Do me a favor, will you? It's easy."

Walker said nothing, waiting.

"Show me you can still smile and stay sane. Show me those pearly whites."

What Walker managed was more like a grimace than a smile, but his lips peeled back enough to show the two large fangs he'd grown to accent his perfect white tombstone teeth.

WALKER

"IT'S MY FAULT," WALKER REPEATED.

Reginald stood up slowly. "I see that," he said. He took a step back. Maurice stepped mostly in front of him.

"I couldn't help myself. It was like I was outside of my body, watching myself do terrible things. I was so hungry." He looked at Reginald, pleading. "*So hungry*, Reggie! I didn't want to do it. I just woke up and all I could feel was hunger, and I knew what I could do. I knew it like instinct. Rutherford was down the hall, running from the others. I just thought, and suddenly, in an instant, I'd gone down the hall and I was behind him, ripping him apart. It didn't take any effort at all. It was like he was made of straw."

Reginald looked at Nikki. She put a hand on his. She knew what it was like to have thirst so intense that she could barely control it. But unlike Walker, Nikki had trained before being turned — mentally as much as physically. She knew how to step back, how to divorce herself from the raw feeling of need. She'd developed her will and knew what she'd be facing. Walker hadn't had any training. One day he was a son of a bitch, and the next day he was a son of a bitch who was incredibly strong, incredibly fast, and incredibly hungry.

Outside, there was a strobe of red light, followed by a strobe of blue. Reginald's head turned. The police had arrived from Walker's 911 call. They were stepping out of their cars, visible through the window. Reginald watched as they drew guns and began pointing flashlights.

"I can smell it," said Walker. "I can still smell blood." His fanged teeth opened and closed. His eyes tried to roll up into his head.

"They're police," said Reginald. "Control yourself. Fight it down."

In a streak of color, Walker was out of the closet and down the hall. Maurice was faster. He caught Walker and threw him back, down the entire length of the hall. Walker struck the water cooler, which exploded like a giant water balloon. Then Nikki was on him, but Walker put a hand on Nikki's chest and pushed, and she crashed through the wall and into the kitchen, where she struck the table and collapsed it. The five coffee cups shattered in a scarlet rain.

Reginald, who couldn't move fast, stood to block the hallway. How many times had Walker slammed him into the walls of this very corridor and complained that he was too wide of a load? It was time to see if Reginald could use that girth to his advantage.

Walker hit Reginald with the momentum of a truck. Reginald didn't come close to standing his ground. Together, they slammed into the plaster wall beside the Xerox machine, Reginald's back striking the wall without pain, cutting out a Reginald shape and cracking the studs.

"Fight it down, you son of a bitch!" Reginald yelled. But Walker wasn't himself. Or maybe he was more himself than he'd ever been in his human life. His face worked. He was like an animal.

Walker was just tensing to flee — to run outside and drain the policemen — when Reginald felt a jolt and found Walker suddenly immobile. He looked to the side and saw a shiny metal shaft connecting Walker's shoulder to one of the wall studs.

Reginald ducked out from between Walker and the wall. Walker started to struggle, but suddenly he was just a man pinned down with what appeared to be a giant fork used for turning hot dogs on a grill — probably from this summer's company picnic. He was, again, only human.

When Reginald came around to Walker's back, he noticed a shiny metal object hanging out of the wound where the barbecue fork had entered Walker's shoulder. It was the late Clara Norris's crucifix, which she never failed to wear around her neck every day of her adult life, on a long chain of pure sliver.

Maurice stood behind Walker, nodding with satisfaction. He looked up, through the window, at the policemen entering the building. But first things first. He placed one of his hands on each side of Walker's head and prepared to twist it off. But before he could, Nikki held up a hand.

"Wait," she said.

"What?" said Maurice. Walker was wriggling, trying to free himself.

"He can't help it. He wasn't prepared. Believe me, I know what it feels like."

Maurice's fangs were out. The expression on his face was like the snarl of a wolf.

"He's a murderer," he said.

"Aren't *you*?"

Maurice looked at Nikki. "He's a wildcard in a society increasingly filled with wildcards. And what's more, he's nearly as hurt, mentally, as those he's murdered. Killing him would be a mercy."

Nikki stared daggers at him. "No," she said.

Maurice gave Reginald a look, asking for help.

"He's not going anywhere with that silver against his blood," said Reginald. It wasn't help. It wasn't even an answer. But it was the best he could do, because even though he wanted Walker dead as badly as Maurice did, he saw Nikki's point. He could tell how much of herself she saw in the monster in front of them.

"Look," Reginald continued, reading Maurice's face. "Let's go talk to the police. You can watch Walker if you want. Let's think this out. And if we have to, in the end, we can always still kill him."

After a minute, Maurice made a small, pained nod.

Reginald made jazz hands at Nikki. "Showtime," he said.

COPS

REGINALD AND NIKKI MADE IT as far as the lobby before encountering four men with drawn weapons.

Nikki had unbuttoned her shirt an extra two buttons to lubricate the conversation — something Reginald had told her not to do because she was bound to embarrass herself. Nikki was effortlessly sexy, meaning that she was sexy at all times other than when she was trying to be. So when she arrived in the lobby, she leaned on a doorframe, arched her back, and pushed her chest out. She licked her lips and made a comment about how the office party had gotten hot enough to call firemen. Realizing her mistake, she corrected herself by saying "I mean, hot enough to call *police*men," but then slapped herself on the forehead because that was stupid and didn't make sense. The sudden movement caused one of the policemen to shoot her.

The policeman who shot her was a plainclothes detective at the front of the group. He was a tall man with gray hair at the temples. In a movie, his character would be killed one day before retirement, but the detective apparently knew about and was determined to avoid the cliche through any means necessary. After shooting Nikki, he yelled at her to get down on the ground — something pain had mostly caused her to do already. Nikki seemed to find this treatment unfair, but Reginald could understand where the cops were coming from. Sexy or not, Nikki was covered head to toe with blood.

The police didn't seem to have noticed Reginald while they were busy subduing the hot, bloody brunette with the exposed bra. He started to back away, but then one of the uniformed cops saw the message written on the elevator in blood. Reginald locked eyes with the cop and raised his hands, but the cop shot him in the face anyway.

"You guys all need to work on your impulse control," said Reginald from the floor. The bullet had knocked him down and ripped open the back of his throat, but fortunately he still wasn't feeling pain.

"Stand down!" yelled the detective, as if he hadn't fired one of the shots himself. Reginald couldn't see the detective because he'd spun as he'd fallen, but the voice Reginald heard suggested that that the speaker was snarling. Imagining the snarl, Reginald realized he'd already concocted a whole imaginary backstory for the detective: He was a seasoned pro who did everything by the books, but he'd been saddled with a loose cannon of a partner in his final days on the force. He liked his coffee with two packets of equal and a spoonful of that shitty powdered creamer. He had a boat named SEA WHISPERER.

A toe nudged Reginald. He turned, then came up onto his knees. A weapon was pointed at his face. Reginald looked past the gun and saw that the three other cops were occupied. One was looking uneasily at the ONLY HUMAN message on the elevator, one was peeking past Reginald into what had to look like a carnival of horrors, and the detective was still covering Nikki.

"It's fine," Reginald told the cop. "You missed me."

The cop's mouth was hanging open. His gun was shaking. Slowly, Reginald reached up and ran two fingers across his cheek. They came away bright red. Then he looked over his shoulder and saw a huge blossom of what used to be his blood and brains.

Reginald sighed and looked the cop in the eyes. "All right, we'll do this the easy way," he said. "Holster your weapon."

The cop shrugged and slid his gun into its holster.

The detective looked over. He seemed alarmed until Reginald met his eyes and said, "That sounds like a good idea. Let's all put down our weapons and talk this out."

The detective blinked at him, then pursed his lips thoughtfully. "That sounds like a good idea. Let's all put down our weapons and talk this out," he said. Then he flicked the safety on the side of his own gun and put it away.

One of the two remaining men looked from the detective, to Reginald, to the blood splatter behind him, to the elevators, and then repeated the circuit.

The eyes of the last man became locked in Reginald's gaze. A moment later, he holstered his weapon and said to the still-unglamoured cop, "I've always loved you."

The final policeman looked at the other three, incredulous. There was a moment of tense indecision, but then he looked at Reginald, seemed to relax, and put his own gun away.

"Rough night, huh?" said Reginald, standing up. He looked over at Nikki, who, fully healed, walked over to sit on the lobby bench.

"Rough night," the detective agreed.

"First things first," said Reginald. "You came here and found that we were all drunk and that the call to 911 was a prank. If you get any phone calls about missing people who work in this office, you'll tell them that you responded to a call here and found the people they're calling about drunk or passed out and that you... I don't know... hauled them off to the drunk tank. Do cops still do that?"

"I've always loved you," repeated one of the uniformed cops.

"If you hear from anyone who came here looking for someone and found dead people, you'll think they're hysterical." He thought for a moment, then added, "'Hysterical' like *crazy*, not like funny."

"Good catch," said Nikki. "That could have been awkward."

Reginald looked from the eyes of one man to another, to the third, to the fourth. "When, eventually, your fellow policemen discover that something untoward actually did happen here and you can no longer deny it, you'll remember everything you saw — except that you won't remember me or this woman. We weren't here, and you didn't talk to us. You came in and found everyone dead. You will remember that the traumatic nature of what you saw threw you into some sort of post-traumatic state and caused... temporary amnesia, I guess."

"Nobody will buy that," said the detective. "I've been through too much to go into post-trauma after seeing some bodies."

This was a new and very helpful thing that Reginald had discovered as his glamouring skills developed. Not only was he increasingly able to "second-hand glamour" people he never met by using people he did, but his subjects more and more often pointed out logical flaws and holes in Reginald's glamour stories. Once, a man Nikki had brought home for Reginald to feed on had asked him, "How did my pants go missing at a Tony Robbins seminar?" during his final debrief. (The man's pantsless state hadn't fazed Reginald, which was troubling in itself.) So Reginald had concocted a side story involving a bachelorette party in the hotel where Nikki had found the man, where Tony Robbins had also been Unleashing the Power Within a few thousand people.

Reginald took two steps forward, reared back, and punched the detective hard enough to throw him into the opposite wall. The detective rebounded off the drywall but stayed on his feet.

Reginald pointed at one of the other cops. "That guy over there slammed your car door on your head while you were here. It gave you a concussion and some short-term memory loss. Better?"

"I'm getting too old for this shit," said the detective, rubbing his scalp.

Reginald told the four policemen to walk outside, then followed them through the outer door and into the parking lot. Nikki stood with the five men for two minutes before announcing that she was cold and that her nipples were hard enough to cut glass. She went inside.

Reginald, who'd always had good natural insulation, felt fine despite his lack of a coat. He looked at each of the policemen in turn, then said to the detective, "What are you hearing about all of these killings and disasters lately?"

"We're hearing that there are a lot of them," he replied. "Nobody can keep up."

One of the uniformed cops added, "People are saying it's vampires."

Reginald's eyebrows rose. If the policemen weren't glamoured, that particular tidbit wouldn't have come out even if they'd wanted to discuss their work with Reginald. Even amongst themselves, he doubted any of the cops would admit to believing in monsters, but scared people came up with all sorts of preposterous explanations that they'd never share openly.

"Why vampires?"

The detective, who had apparently heard the same rumors and had access to more case data, answered for him. "Victims are torn apart, often drained of blood. Witnesses have reported seeing people run away in a flash, jump impossibly high, pick up incredibly heavy objects. A lot of the dead appear to have been bitten on the necks — twin punctures through the carotid artery."

"Don't you think it's more likely that it's the work of psychopaths?" said Reginald.

"We'd like to believe that, but it's getting harder and harder to."

"Why?"

"It's too widespread. It's too coordinated. Too many people are dying in the same exact way. Whatever's doing this is too strong and too fast. There are too many strange eyewitness accounts to be coincidence. And it's happening everywhere — all over the country, and maybe even outside of the country."

"One of the men's wives made these for the entire department," said one of the patrolmen, reaching into his shirt. He pulled out a small wooden cross on a length of rawhide string. "Everyone laughed and mocked both her and her husband. She's a real bible-beater, this woman. The jokes have been constant, and Harper hasn't had a moment's peace. But recently, everyone is wearing them. Even while they continue to make their jokes."

Reginald reached out and took the cross in his hand. It was crude and done without craftsmanship, as if it had been made in a hurry. Then he looked into the eyes of each man in turn.

"Silver," he said. "Replace them with *silver* crosses, on silver chains."

One of the patrolmen put his hand on Reginald's shoulder. "I've always loved you," he said.

BREAKDOWN

THEY WERE IN A DARK car. There was no moon.

In the back seat, Maurice sat next to Todd Walker. He'd wrapped the silver crucifix chain twice around Walker's neck and had told him that even without the silver, he was much faster and much stronger than Walker could imagine. He added that he was absolutely dying to twist Walker's head off like the lid of a mayo jar, so giving him an excuse to do so wouldn't be wise.

Reginald was driving. Nikki sat in the passenger seat beside him, her face concerned. Every once in a while, she'd turn to look out the side window for minutes at a time and say nothing. The radio had been off earlier, but Nikki had turned it on because she said that silence made the mood too eerie. The volume was low. It was set to a country music station, and during the breaks between songs, the deejays kept talking about calamities that had occurred this week and comparing them to calamities that had occurred last week. Was this week's mass unexplained college campus killing fundamentally different from the mass unexplained industrial park killings last week? Were things improving or getting worse in given parts of the city? How did the roving rape gangs downtown (which had been operating for weeks) compare with the new roving rape gangs that seemed to be gaining ground in Hilliard? The deejays wondered (in the "why, cruel world?" way that people wondered, more lamenting than actually pondering) what was going on with the world. A caller jokingly mentioned vampires, and another slightly hysterical (again, *crazy*-hysterical rather than *funny*-hysterical) caller theorized that this was the beginning of the end, and that the gates of Hell were swinging wide to allow demons to walk the earth.

It was like listening to *War of the Worlds,* minus the aliens, with a southern accent.

The picture painted by the police detectives had set Reginald's mind on edge. The deejay chatter wasn't helping. Incidents like the one at the office were happening everywhere, it seemed, and the detective Reginald had glamoured had said that it was becoming increasingly difficult to come up with logical explanations for them. The forensics teams gave the detectives information that didn't make sense. The detectives tried to work with the nonsensical information, and when they did, they came up with explanations that were outlandish but at least seemed rational. They proposed that the culprits were teams of strongmen with wild animals. They proposed that hallucinogenic agents had been released into the water or the air. They proposed that similar events in disparate locations pointed to vast, coordinated gangs of cultists with vampire fetishes, and when they proposed such widespread conspiracies, they called the FBI to report what they'd found and to compare notes, to whatever extent the FBI was willing to share. But as time passed, as more bizarre events occurred, even the crazy-rational explanations ceased. Cases were closed and filed — or perhaps opened and held with the hope that someone might somehow, someday, miraculously find the missing piece and make sense of it all. More cases showed up each week, each day. The cases came in faster than investigators could process them. Cases stacked up and became routine, no longer amazing or terrible. They were simply added to the ongoing roster of atrocities; another day on the job. Police departments everywhere were in triage mode, content to clean up the bodies as quickly as they appeared, even if they couldn't propose an explanation for what had occurred. From what the detectives reported hearing up the chain, the FBI these days wasn't much different.

Reginald gave the policemen back at the office the only help he could. He told them that if they couldn't find silver or wooden bullets — which they wouldn't be able to — that crossbows firing wooden bolts made better weapons than guns of any type or caliber, and that they should always aim for the heart. He told them that they and their friends and families should stay inside their houses after dark whenever they could. He suggested wearing silver jewelry, which might buy them some time, and carrying any lights they could find that mimicked the wavelengths of sunlight.

It was nearly 3am by the time Reginald's car pulled into the alley behind the bagel deli and the group walked down to the Asbury, where the Vampire Council remained and seemed determined to stay.

Nothing had been cleaned up. The lookout was gone from the ticket booth, but the corpses and the blood were still there. Either no police had come looking for whoever the bodies had once been, or — more likely — the police *had* arrived, had been glamoured, and then had gone back to their station to close the books on yet another missing persons case in an untenable slush pile of unsolved missing persons cases.

The club's main room was still mostly empty. The door to the basement was still ajar, and Reginald, as he approached with Nikki, Maurice, and the restrained Todd Walker, could still hear noises coming from below. This time, however, they found a very large vampire bouncer at the top of the stairs. He wasn't there for long. The bouncer was barely able to raise a hand before Maurice leapt at him across the length of the club with a broken-off chair leg in his fist. A second later, all that guarded the door was a pile of ash and clothes, and Maurice's shoulders were rising and falling, and he kicked the ash in frustration before stomping down the steps into total chaos.

The Council had stopped being a Council.

The main arena and surrounding stands had become a throng of bodies. Vampires milled everywhere, turning the overcrowded space into an odd amalgam of marketplace, battle royale, and flophouse. Vampires were huddled in corners and asleep on benches where the assembly normally sat, drunk on drunken humans or — Reginald thought — perhaps high on human junkies, which he'd heard about but had never seen. The stoned vampires resembled human junkies, lying semi-conscious in corners, wan and paler than was usual even for the undead, their eyes distant and dreamy. It was possible, Reginald had heard, to become addicted to drug addicts. It was more psychological than physical, though; human junkies often wanted to quit and couldn't, whereas vampire junkies simply didn't want to quit. Because they were more or less immortal, they had no real reason to.

Human bodies and body parts were everywhere. Reginald almost tripped over an arm walking in. There were drained, paper-skinned humans in corners and in the stands, discarded like empty liquor bottles. The walls and doors were splattered with so much blood that Nikki at first commented that the Council must have redecorated. It smelled like rancid meat. The smell repulsed Reginald, but apparently he was alone; Nikki and Maurice's nostrils flared as they walked in, and Walker tried to tug out of Maurice's grip.

Maurice had to (and wanted to) break his clavicle to keep him still. Walker yelled out in pain, but nobody looked over. The atmosphere was too loud, and there was no shortage of screaming in the arena.

The Guard were present, but none were at their posts. They'd clustered into small groups and stared daggers at Reginald's group as they crossed the floor. Reginald knew what the black groups of Guards were calling themselves from Fangbook. They referred to themselves as Kill Squads, and they did exactly what their name implied. Their function was to do what the Deacon wouldn't — to lead the Vampire Nation in decisive action, massacring until the balance began to tip in their favor. The looks that the Kill Squads gave Reginald's group would best be described as "appraising." They were wondering if enough time had passed in anarchy to allow them to murder the Deacon with impunity. Several bared their fangs.

Everywhere, in every corner, vampires were feeding on humans. Some of these seemed to have been brought in wild and unglamoured. Reginald had to avert his gaze as some of those present toyed with conscious prey, allowing humans run and then blurring past them, confronting them no matter where they went, laughing at their terror.

Nikki's eyes were watery. Her throat was hitching, as if trying to swallow something it couldn't pass. Only once they'd entered the Council room — a tiny oasis in a sea of chaos — did her agitation subside. The walls of the Council room were broken and dirty and bloodied, but the chamber itself was far cleaner than the arena and was mostly empty. The room's emptiness and its relative order were probably due to the work of Brian Nickerson, its sole occupant. Brian was sitting in a chair when they entered, reading a book.

"How can you be sitting here reading?" Nikki practically screamed at him.

"Because I don't want to be out there, and because staring at the walls gets old fast," he answered placidly.

"Why don't you *do* something?" said Maurice, indicating the melee in the arena.

Brian chuckled. "You're the Deacon, Deacon."

Maurice closed his eyes and pinched the bridge of his nose.

"You don't like the new Council?" said Brian, placing a bookmark in his book and standing up. "See now, I'd forgotten that some people still felt that way. Vampire YouTube and Fangbook love it. They're very eager to vote on things now that they have the power. So between meetings, they've been finding all sorts of other, non-governmental things to vote up and vote down. This chaos? This that you find so repugnant? Hell, they've created it. They've weighed in. They've rocked the vote right and proper."

"What have they been voting on?" said Reginald.

Brian rubbed his chin. Reginald couldn't tell if he was trying to make an ironic point or if he was genuinely nonplussed by what the Vampire Council had become.

"They particularly enjoy pageants," Brian said after a meditative pause. "The way it works is, they bring in four or five humans and they line them up. Then they broadcast photos and video to the Net, and Fangbook votes on what happens to the humans, in what order. A lot of the 'contestants' are turned. Others are... well, *not* turned."

Walker fidgeted in Maurice's grasp. Maurice dragged him to the other end of the small room and sat him heavily in a metal chair. Then, after reminding Walker that he'd live only as long as Maurice decreed he'd live, Maurice removed the silver chain from his neck and used it to tie him to a heavy iron pipe.

"Care to introduce your friend?" said Brian, watching Maurice work.

"He's a co-worker," said Maurice. "This is a project we're working on together for a client."

"So you brought him in, so that he could see the show?" Then Brian pitched his voice to Walker, whose head was down, his face invisible. "Sorry, co-worker," he said. "Council is usually more organized and impressive than this. It's too bad you couldn't see it as Reginald saw it the first time." Then Brian tossed a tension-breaking smile in Reginald's direction. The first time Reginald had seen the Council, he had been on trial for his life.

"*Someone* wouldn't let me kill him, and he's too dangerous to have loose. He needs to learn vampirism from vampires," said Maurice, returning to the group. He looked at Walker. Then he looked through the door and into the arena, shaking his head. "But if these are to be his role models, I think I might have to kill him after all."

"I'm sorry, Maurice," said Brian, sighing.

Nikki's carefully set facial expression finally broke.

"You're sorry. You're *sorry?* Open killing! Open defiance! Breaches of protocol, drunkenness and depravity, harvesting humans for humiliation and torture? All of that, and you just sit here, reading and making jokes? Why haven't you done anything, Councilman Nickerson?"

"What do you suggest I do, Nikki?"

"Anything," she said. "Anything! Talk to the others. Get them to see reason."

"*Reason.*" Brian laughed. "Did you know that there's a huge movement right now that's read a deadline into the Ring of Fire incident? It's like those nutjobs who said the world would end in 2012. I don't know when this supposed Ring of Fire armageddon date is exactly, but I will say, from watching them, that a deadline really is a fantastic motivator. You thought they were dangerous before? Now they're dangerous *on a deadline*. Dangerous, and crazy, and scared out of their motherfucking minds, pardon my French. You can't talk reason into people who are panicking."

"Try."

But Reginald answered for him, addressing Nikki in his calmest tone of voice.

"Right now, Brian is our insider, and the one person here who can provide a counterpoint to the craziest of the ideas that come to vote. He'll be that as long as he doesn't rock the boat, but you saw what it's like out there. The moment he tries to push any sort of an agenda — any agenda at all — they'll oust him at best, or kill him at worst."

Brian gave a nod. "That's about the size of it," he said.

"So we just give up?" said Nikki.

"No," said Maurice. "We may indeed have to give up, but I'm not going to give up without at least trying to make a last stand."

"You want to *fight?*" said Brian, his face incredulous.

But Reginald, thanks to their shared blood, could read Maurice in a way that Brian couldn't.

"No," said Reginald. "He wants to speak."

SPEECH

MAURICE DIDN'T TAKE THE BACK set of stairs to the Deacon's box. Instead, he walked through the front door of the Council room, crossed the clay-floored arena, and took the steps that ran up through the stands.

Everyone recognized the Deacon, even amidst the chaos. The first few who saw him climbing the steps turned, fangs out and bloody from feeding, snarls on their lips, and watched their lame duck leader as he went by, his eyes steely and forward. Reginald, arm-in-arm with Nikki, followed in Maurice's wake. Malice seemed to press down on them like a giant, suffocating hand. Then, as the first few turned, others followed their gaze. Soon the entire assembly was watching as the thin, shallow-chested, black-haired vampire passed, trailed by his large companion and the beautiful brunette.

Each watcher seemed to be weighing a decision. They wanted to challenge Maurice and his defunct authority, but Maurice was many times older, stronger, and faster than all of them. So they watched, and they waited.

When Maurice reached the box, he lowered himself regally in the large sandstone throne. By now, all of the vampires with present minds (and even a few of the junkies, who were largely absent) were quiet, watching the Deacon. Maurice raised a large stone and struck it against the arm of the throne. Then he stood and called the Assembly to order. Nobody moved; nobody went to their seats; nobody cleared the crowded arena floor or filed into place in the Council box. Reginald could see several Council members, including Charles himself, in the crowd. They looked up at the Deacon's box with scorn.

Nobody moved. Everyone was watching. There had to be four or five hundred of them on the floor, in the seats, in every corner. Other than Brian Nickerson, there wasn't a friendly face among them.

Maurice took a deep breath, then spoke.

"I am not blind," he said. "I know that the office I hold means very little now, and will likely mean nothing at all very soon. The Vampire Nation has spoken. It has chosen a farce of democracy over a sovereign leader. In the days of Logan, I would have applauded the change. Even today, had certain events not occurred, I would have applauded it. I did not want to be your leader. I would not have seized power if there had been another way to save the lives of my progeny and his progeny. But our rules said that after I deposed Logan, I was the one who had to lead this Council and this Nation. But I did not want the power I was given, and today, that power means nothing, which means that I am free. Congratulations. The Vampire Nation is now a nation by the vampires, for the vampires. We crossed the seas centuries ago in crates of dirt, and now we are free to live the American dream, free to determine our own futures, free from autocratic rule."

He paused, scanning the crowd. Then he said, "The Vampire Nation does not need a despot. It does not need a Deacon. But it does need a *leader*. You think you are able to determine your own path without the help of an authority, but you are not. You need someone to tell you what to do. I have spent two millennia watching the humans on this planet, and I have watched the humans of this country during my centuries here — centuries more than most of you in attendance have been alive. It is *not* every man for himself. It is *not* every man and woman created equal. There are privileged classes. There are those who are above the law and those who live beneath its heel. Their system is not perfect, but it works because there has always been someone in charge — someone who tells the others what to do. Some agree with that leader and some disagree. Some follow the rules and some willfully disobey them. But the rules *exist*. The rules are always *there*, as a benchmark to obey or to rebel against. The leader is always there, as a person to follow or oppose. The enemy is always there too, even though the enemy is manufactured by those in charge. There is always something that the people are told to hate and something that the people are told to love. There is always a threat the people are told to fear. And on one level, it's wrong, and it's false. But on another level, a defined — if false — good and bad and right and wrong gives the people a way to orient themselves. You can believe that the enemy is truly an enemy or you can disbelieve it, just the same as you can agree with the leader or disagree. But the enemy is *there*. The fear is *there*. And so what the humans have — here, and everywhere — is a carefully constructed artificial reality. It's not real. It's designed to manipulate. But regardless of all of the bad things it is, it is still a system. It is still a single point of focus for all of those people, regardless how they behave relative to it. And the system, for all the negative, artificial, manipulative things it is, is tolerable. The system, whether it is good or evil or right or wrong or real or artificial, is something that a person can live within and survive. Inside of the system, true freedom is blunted... but so is true slavery. True peace is hard to come by... but true chaos is hard to come by as well. True peace of mind is nearly nonexistent... but within the system, true terror is nonexistent as well."

The crowd continued to watch Maurice, its attention absolute.

"Right now, the Vampire Nation faces a crisis. You are on the brink of true freedom — both from the restrictions of a government, but also from its protection. And I'm here to say to you: *You cannot handle true freedom.* You are not ready. You have proven it, both here in this room and out in the world. A system would lie to you, but most of you still need the lie. Most of you cannot handle the unblunted horror of what we are facing. You cannot handle your true natures. Philosophers have debated the nature of humanity — whether in the absence of socialization, humans are innately good and kind or innately animalistic and cruel. But there is no debating the true nature of a vampire. We are killers. We don't create life; we end life. We do not build; we destroy. We do not grow; we hunt. In older countries, vampires have come to know their natures, and they have built their own systems, to lie to themselves and contain that nature. But you have never had to do this. You are used to having someone else define reality for you. You are used to having someone tell you what to do. You are used to someone telling you what to fear and what not to fear. Right now, you are afraid. *You need a leader to lie to you and tell you that everything will be all right.*

"I do not want to lead you as Deacon," said Maurice. "But I want to help you to find a democratic leader. I want to help this Nation to grow a new head rather than to run around headless. Take my power away from me. It's fine. But allow me to help you put some of that power back into the right pair of hands. Let me help you keep the center together, to find a lie that will support you rather than destroy you, and then I will step aside. This Nation is sliding into chaos. This Nation is sliding into anarchy and self-determinism, and I say again, *You are not ready.* Left to your own devices, you are terrible. You are evil. You cannot truly determine what to do on your own."

Maurice stopped speaking, and it took Reginald a moment to realize that he was finished.

"Give them a call to action," said Reginald.

"I'd like to suggest a law to the Council," said Maurice. He pointed at Brian, speaking to him directly. "Construct an election process. Make it fair and impossible to cheat. You don't want me as your leader? Fine. Find a leader amongst you that suits you. But *find a leader.*"

Brian stood. "I propose a law to do what he says. Any objections?"

"Yes," said a voice from the floor. "I object to the idea that vampires cannot decide for themselves, and I'd like to propose an alternative course of action to what the esteemed Deacon has suggested."

It was Charles. Behind him were row after row of black-helmeted Council Guard.

MAXIMUM MOTHERFUCKING KUNG-FU

CHARLES AND THE GUARD ADVANCED, pushing aside the milling vampires on the arena floor. It had to be all of the Guard — the entire contingent, all in one place.

"Guards," said Charles, "please take the Deacon and the pretty woman behind him into custody so that we can kill them as painfully as possible. If they resist, go ahead and kill them outright. Maurice may be old, but he can't take on all of you."

It was true. Real life wasn't like a kung fu movie, where attackers were kind enough to come on one or two at a time. If the Guard all came for Maurice, he might kill a few of them but then would be overwhelmed.

The Guard captain next to Charles said something to him.

Charles replied, loud enough for the whole room to hear, "Don't worry about the fat one. I'd like to handle that bit of unpleasantness myself." He reached behind his back and retrieved something that he then held in his fist like a threat. Reginald looked closer. It was a sharpened wooden stake.

Then, in one blurring motion, Charles struck. He didn't precisely *jump* from the arena floor up to the Deacon's box. It was more like he was *fired* from the floor. He struck Reginald in the chest, and his momentum threw the Charles/Reginald ball toward the back of the box. Maurice and Nikki turned to react, but the Guard were already advancing, climbing the stands and the walls and the catwalks above like swarming spiders. Maurice's head twitched in the dozen directions from which the Guard were coming, but there was nothing to do as they slowly surrounded him. They were taking their time. Maurice and Nikki were pinned in place. Any one of them could strike at any time.

And then something worse began to happen. The rest of the vampires in the arena began to rise behind the Guard. They got to their feet; they marched slowly up the steps and through the stands. Reginald could hear every seat creaking, every body stirring. Every one of the hundreds of vampires in the building was coming at them. And every vampire on Fangbook was watching, surely betting on who would die first.

Charles effortlessly pinned Reginald to the floor with one hand. Reginald's strength was no match for Charles's. Charles didn't hesitate. He raised the spike, eyeing Reginald's face and then a spot in the middle of his chest.

"Maurice and I made you, our little mistake, together," said Charles. "But the difference is that

I'm willing to admit my mistake and correct it." And then he drove the stake home, into Reginald's heart.

But when the stake struck Reginald's chest, it shredded into thousands of tiny bits. Charles's fist became a forest of splinters — some large and some small — and he screamed.

"Seriously," said Reginald. "I'm the first vampire to ever think of this?" He raised the bottom of his shirt to show Charles the chain mail vest that he, like Nikki and Maurice, had been wearing for months. Then, focusing all of his strength into his arms, he gave a shove and rolled his superior girth onto his attacker, pinning Charles beneath him. Charles was strong, but he weighed half of what Reginald weighed and was at a temporary disadvantage, too pained by the hundreds of wood shards in his fist to react.

Then, to buy himself a few more seconds, Reginald kneed Charles in the testicles.

He focused on the chaos around him.

Everything stopped. The arena became a still-life.

Reginald looked around, knowing that what felt like movement of his head was just a trick of perception. He saw it all. He filed and processed the position of every one of the hundreds of people in the room. Within his awareness, he had all the time he'd need to analyze it. He could see every piece of the massive, interlocking puzzle that the Council under the Asbury had become.

The closest Guards were fifteen feet from Maurice. None had weapons. Weapons would get in the way. If there were still snipers at the ring of windows around the top of the arena, they might fire, but their chain mail vests made the wooden bullets irrelevant. The Guards, on the other hand, would simply use their hands and teeth to tear Maurice's head off — something the chain mail did nothing to prevent. Maurice would be able to take down a few of them, but there were already seven within striking distance and two distinct waves behind them.

In Reginald's still-life, the Guard at the front of the advancing pack had his hands hooked into claws. His fangs were out, the tips wet with blood. Maurice was standing his ground, his feet planted, his arms out, ready to spring in any direction. But *which* direction? Two Guards were coming from his right, two were coming from his left, and one was directly in front of him. One Guard was advancing from behind, and there was even one in the rafters, preparing to drop from above.

Nikki didn't seem to be the primary target, but she was right next to Maurice. The eyes of at least one of the Guard were on her. Her own eyes, interestingly, were on Reginald. No matter where he seemed to move in his still-life, her eyes seemed to follow him like a trick painting. She must be actually looking right at him, wherever they were relative to each other in real time. He could see fear in her eyes, but it wasn't fear for herself. It was fear for Reginald. He looked back to what the moment had been before he'd entered hyper-awareness. Reginald had just rolled over onto Charles. It couldn't have been more than five seconds earlier that Charles had tried to stake him.

Nikki's eyes on his. His eyes looking into Nikki's.

Reginald suddenly felt angry. It was a hot, indignant kind of anger, totally unlike the panicky, tantrum-style anger that he usually felt. And with that thought, he realized that what he was feeling wasn't his own anger. He was feeling Nikki's anger, just as she sometimes felt the thirst of others in her bloodline.

What you're feeling is blood ties, Maurice had told her.

Reginald tried to focus on Nikki, on her blood, on his own blood, on the bond that they shared as maker and progeny.

Nikki, he thought. *Extend your index finger.*

Reginald allowed his mental focus to slip. The still-life around him ground slowly forward, like a carousel on a rusty spindle. The Guard who were advancing at human speeds in real time moved now at a pace that was barely perceptible. Two vampires in the distance who'd run for the door looked as if they were jogging, but were doing so with the posture of sprinters. Maurice's head had been flicking around as he watched the Guard approach, and Reginald saw it now as if Maurice were in a very interesting art gallery. He looked here, there, up, down.

At the end of Nikki's right hand, her index finger flicked out like the blade on a switchblade.

Reginald focused, and again the world ground to a halt.

He thought. Fortunately, he had all the time in the world to do it.

You're trapped, said an internal voice. *The fact that you can analyze every detail of your trap changes nothing.*

And that was totally true. If a Guard came at him, Reginald could stop and think about it for as long as he wanted, but the moment he stopped concentrating, his internal clock would sync with reality and the Guard would be on him. He hadn't gotten any faster or stronger. If he tried to run, he'd easily be overtaken.

Nikki and Maurice, on the other hand, were strong and fast. If they were able to do what he could do with his mind, they'd be able to pause to analyze, then resume and react, then repeat. But they couldn't.

There has to be a way to use this.

How? said the skeptical voice. *You'll only be able to watch in excruciating detail as all of you are overtaken and die.*

Reginald closed his eyes, which in itself was a mental device because in reality, his eyes were open. He focused on Nikki, feeling her in his veins like a presence within him. And he thought, *Nikki.*

Behind you, to your right side, three feet from Maurice's left arm, there's a Guard with his hands high, about to jump. Come in low, below his arms.

Reginald, getting the feel for this time-stop concentration thing, defocused and watched as everything ground to slow life around him. A Guard to Maurice's right came another step forward. The running vampires near the entrance vanished through the door. Nikki swiveled with surprising speed, squatted like a boxer coming in for an uppercut, and drove her fist through the chest of the advancing Guard.

Reginald focused, and everything stopped. He could see Nikki's knuckles emerging from the Guard's back, but what was spraying out wasn't blood. It was grayer, and there were sparks. Then Reginald remembered that Nikki wore an African ring on that hand, which was carved out of polished wood.

Reginald made a mental note that another must-have item for the well-equipped vampire soldier of today would be wooden knuckles, not unlike brass knuckles.

Maurice's head had turned, despite the dozens now advancing on him. His brows were furrowed. The expression on his face was one of curiosity, as if he'd heard a noise he couldn't explain.

Maurice, pick me up.

Although Reginald was the brain, he was none of the brawn. If he was to participate in this lopsided battle, he'd need to do it as a backpack worn by someone who was much faster than he was.

Time resumed. Maurice turned and, without hesitation, came to where Reginald was laying and hoisted him over one shoulder as if he weighed nothing at all. Even at the glacial pace Reginald was allowing, Maurice's movement was blurred.

Jesus, is he fast.

Time stopped.

Nikki, come with us, he thought.

She turned.

It's a game of chess — just a very big, very complex game of chess, Reginald thought. *Assess the pieces. Anticipate the moves of hundreds of simultaneous opponents twenty steps in advance. Win, or die.*

They began to make their way down the front stairway. It was tempting to tell Maurice to jump to the arena floor, but the pauses and slow-downs were an illusion that existed solely within Reginald's mind. Nothing was actually stopping or slowing, and the same laws as ever applied in real time. One of those laws said that vampires were much faster than gravity. In the time it would take for them to fall through the air and land, they could have twenty Guards on them.

The process required tremendous concentration and was incredibly stressful. Reginald couldn't hear the others because they couldn't think as fast as he could, so he was on his own to mastermind their fight and hopeful escape.

It felt like he was moving pieces around inside of a giant diorama, but he could only go forward, never backward. The relative speeds and strength of all three of them still applied. He had to make guesses and anticipate where others were moving, but if they got backed into a corner, they'd still be backed into a corner — no matter how slowly it happened.

Reginald sweated each move. The pause-think-resume-act cycle made it easier to see what to do, but whether opportunities presented themselves or not still depended a lot on luck. The walls could easily still close in, and if they did, it might actually be *more* terrible to watch them close in slowly than it would have been in real time.

Ahead of them, two vampires — roughnecks who were not Guard, and who looked like recently turned members of a biker gang, were crouched in their way. Reginald had been watching them. In a second, they'd spring forward, launching themselves in the air at Maurice and Nikki's necks. Evading them was as simple. Reginald told Maurice to drop him, then to grab him by the leg and drag him. He told both Maurice and Nikki to go onto their hands and knees and scamper forward, staying low. By the time the pair jumped, Maurice and Nikki were already on the floor, moving underneath them with Reginald in tow. The vampires soared harmlessly above them. Reginald had time to notice paired looks of perplexity on their faces. Then Maurice hoisted Reginald onto his back and resumed running.

They dodged. They evaded. Heads were pulled off. As long as they could keep space around them, they'd be okay. A halo of three feet was enough to maneuver as long as no more than two or three vampires were ever inside of it. Maurice was fast enough to outrun any claw or fang, and even Nikki, who was millennia younger, had been born with enough prowess to punch through two attackers in the time it would take one to strike her, as long as she knew exactly where to strike, how to strike, and when.

Reginald steered them through tangles of arms and bodies, propelled them over scrums, turned them into precision weapons.

Then Reginald remembered Maurice's sword. He wore it all the time unless it was taken from him, and the Guard hadn't taken it today because the Guard had deserted their posts.

Maurice unsheathed his weapon.

Choke up on it, thought Reginald.

There wasn't enough room in the crowd to swing a sword without getting tangled and losing time to the momentum of big swings, so Maurice grabbed the sword in its middle, his hand immediately cutting and bleeding crimson against its razor edge. He gripped it tightly, the blade stopping and anchoring once it became wedged in bone. Then he started to swing it with one hand like a double-ended axe, slicing and swiping with both ends.

The handle on one end of the sword was unwieldy, so Maurice broke it off as simply as snapping a twig. Then, even in a life-and-death situation, even while they were outnumbered by more than a hundred to each of their one, Reginald had to laugh inside of his head as he watched Maurice swing with one hand while using the other to stow the handle of the sword in his pants pocket, so that he could have it fixed later if they survived.

It would normally have been impossible for Maurice, even as fast as he was, to deliver perfect neck shots with each swipe of the sword, but Reginald guided him through each swing, having him adjust higher or lower, far end up or far end down, even once he'd begun to strike. Each time a head came off, gravity took over. Because gravity was the slowest force in the room, they had to dodge what looked like stationary, floating heads as they cut through the crowd. Reginald decided that clearing heads was something he could handle, even as slow as he was. So from atop Maurice's shoulders, he began using his own glacial hands to slap them away as they began to flake into dust. As he did, Reginald made a mental note to watch the video of this if they made it out alive. In real time, what they were doing had to look like vegetables being fed into a food processor.

There was a knot of vampires in front of them. Too many to cut through. They were too dense, without sufficient room to cut or strike or evade. Reginald's mind looked to the left. A gap was closing. He looked to the right, which opened into the Council room. That way was clear, but it would be a dead end, and in the opposite direction from the exit. They couldn't go inside the room unless they wanted to make a last stand using the door as a bottleneck. Reginald did a quick mental calculation. There were still too many of them left. Their chances of killing all of the vampires that remained, even in a bottleneck, were nil. And what was more, Reginald's mind was getting tired. He willed himself into focus, but he couldn't sustain this level of concentration for much longer.

He told Maurice and Nikki to turn left, skirting the crowd. They did. He looked right and saw the wall of vampires. He looked left, now back toward the stands and the Deacon's box, and saw scores cascading down from the seats and rafters. They'd been running for three to five seconds in real time — plenty long enough for everyone to catch on, and plenty long enough for all of those interested in fighting to fight.

The gaps in front of them were beginning to close.

Reginald's mind looked backward, wondering if the open door to the Council room was the wisest choice after all. But even now, it might be too late.

174

A young-looking vampire came in from the right, his hands up and reaching for Reginald, his fangs out. In the same moment, a female vampire was crouched on the floor in front of them. A third had its hands two feet from Nikki.

He told Maurice to strike the closest vampire and told Nikki exactly where and how to disarm the crouching one with a kick. Time rolled forward. All three vampires advanced. The leaping one leapt. Nikki struck it below the chin hard enough to open a stress wound in its neck. Maurice took out the one on his right with his blade. The third advanced a foot, its fingers now very near Nikki's neck.

Nikki, turn to your left! thought Reginald. *Strike with your left hand!*

But her left hand was at her side, and would never make it in time. He changed his order.

Duck!

Time inched forward. The clawed hands came closer. Maurice, having finished his kill, turned. The one Nikki had kicked now had a red line at its neck, its head snapped far enough to touch its head to its back. It's body was arched in the air, starting to flip.

Reginald told Maurice what to do, but Maurice's hands and blade were still to his right.

Reginald thought. All he could do was to wait and see if Maurice could make it, or if Nikki could duck in time.

He inched time forward.

Nikki ducked a few inches, but the vampire was descending on her, and its attack arc followed her ducking motion. Maurice was fast, but not fast enough — and thanks to Nikki and her attacker's downward motion, he would strike too high if he got there in time to strike at all.

Reginald told Nikki to turn away. He tried to kick at the attacker himself.

Time inched forward. The hands touched Nikki's neck. From where Reginald was atop Maurice's shoulders, he could do nothing but watch helplessly.

Everything stopped.

Nikki was going to die. There was nothing he could do. Nothing Nikki could do. Nothing Maurice could do.

A small opening had begun to form in front of them, and beyond the opening was the door to the exit. If Maurice's next move took him forward, he might be able to make it through. But that would mean leaving Nikki behind.

In timelessness, Reginald looked at Nikki. He pondered. He calculated. He prayed.

There was nothing he could do.

It took him a long, long time to reach the inescapable conclusion that either she would die alone or they would all die together. So with great, great, sorrowful reluctance, he commanded Maurice to move toward the exit.

But when time rolled forward again, something massive struck Nikki's attacker from the rear and the encroaching vampire flew away, fast and hard enough even in slow-time to strike the far wall and break into pieces like a ceramic doll. Reginald couldn't bring himself to stop; he allowed his awareness to inch forward so that he could watch it happen.

The massive thing coming up from behind was Brian Nickerson, who was making a berserker run from the Council chamber toward the door.

Reginald had always imagined that Brian must be incredibly powerful given his six-foot-seven, three-hundred-plus pound body made of pure muscle, and he wasn't disappointed. Vampirism had magnified Brian's already-Herculean strength and the surprising speed and agility he'd spent hours each day honing. Brian moved like a wide receiver and cleared bodies like a lineman. He was cutting through the crowd like a train, his head down, his powerful arms tossing bodies aside as if they were tufts of dust. Nothing could stand in his way.

Brian was shameless in his self-preservation. As he stormed forward, Reginald could see that he was holding one of his Council rivals in front of him. His makeshift shield was slashed, cut, bitten, ripped. And when that vampire was mostly spent, Brian started to use him as a club, swinging him around with one hand while he used the other to throw bodies aside.

Reginald didn't waste any time. He directed Nikki and Maurice into Brian's wake, before it closed again with teeth and claws.

Once they were in the corridor, things became easy. Reginald unclenched his tired mental muscles and began watching as things happened in real time. They went up the stairs and through the unguarded lobby. In the blur of a second, they were at the front door. He'd already lost track of Brian, who hadn't so much as looked back. Reginald did look back, slowing time in his mind to do so. The others were coming up from the basement, pouring through the stairwell door and into the Asbury's main room like ocean water rushing through the hull of a sinking ship.

Underneath Reginald, Maurice had stopped. His toe tapped nervously. Nikki was beside them, all three fleeing vampires standing on four feet just past the front door, at the apron of tile in the club's front lobby.

The sun had risen.

It was still low in the sky, casting long shadows across High Street, but the campus buildings to the east side of the road were low, and the shadows wouldn't make for sufficient cover. Sunlight streamed halfway into the Asbury's lobby like a welcome mat made of death. Brian must have run right out into it. If he could find shelter nearby, he might be fine because he was still young. Reginald and Nikki, in theory, could do the same. It would hurt like hell and they wouldn't be able to see where they were going after a while because they'd be blind, but they could do it. Reginald had accidentally fried himself when he was first turned. It had hurt, but a short bout in the sun wouldn't kill a young vampire if he could find shelter quickly and heal.

Maurice, on the other hand, would turn to ash inside of a second.

The vampires from the basement were almost on them. It was a choice between the fat and the fire.

"Nikki," said Reginald. "Take my arms."

She looked down, confused. Reginald had stepped off of Maurice's back and now stood behind him, one hand around each of Maurice's sides, under his armpits. Maurice was short, so Reginald had to crouch to get under his armpits at all.

Nikki took his hands. Reginald then told her to grip higher up on him, so she grabbed his upper arms. Then, when Maurice was between them with their arms gripping each other, she understood. So did Maurice.

"Wait," said Maurice. "No. Don't."

Reginald squeezed Nikki's arms and they both stood up. Maurice hung between their interlocked arms like baggage. Reginald pulled them closer together, creating a Maurice sandwich with Reginald and Nikki bread. Then he rotated them all, turning his back toward the Asbury's front door.

"Come on, you bloodsucker!" he shouted at Maurice. "You wanna live forever?" Then he stepped out into the sun, back first.

The pain was immediate and intense. Reginald didn't understand what brought on his painless state when it came, but he knew that appearances occasionally to the contrary, it wasn't under his conscious control. It wasn't coming now, possibly because he was so exhausted. He could feel every particle of himself beginning to bubble and boil. It was much worse than last time, either because the sun was more direct or because he'd gotten older.

Nikki screamed as a ray stuck her face, creating an immediate welt. Reginald, with all his size, cast a large westward shadow, but it wasn't enough. They had to move, or else they'd die in order — men first.

The vampires from the lobby had reached the demarcation line drawn by the sun. They all stopped, watching the smoking trio in the sun, aghast. Not one of them stepped forward. They wanted the Deacon's blood, but not this badly. In the crowd, Reginald spotted the head of Charles, who looked equally furious and shocked.

"Any time now, Nikki!" said Reginald.

She stopped screaming, made an apologetic noise, then tensed up and arched her back. Reginald felt his feet come off of the ground. The tension between their arms increased as her muscles took on his and Maurice's weight.

Between them, his arms catching sidelong glances of sun and turning black, Maurice groaned.

Then Nikki ran — moving sideways and backward as needed, keeping Reginald's massive and blistering back to the rising sun.

COKE

WHEN DUSK CAME, THEY COULD see it around the edges of the old-fashioned cellar entrance to the bar's basement. The angled basement doors faced west, and for the previous several hours, Nikki had been watching a line of sunlight that came from around its edges as it moved across the concrete floor. Every half hour, she made a mark in the dust, and as the day ended, the lines became farther and farther apart. Finally the direct sun was blocked by buildings on the horizon, and thirty minutes later, the hues around the door's edges turned from yellow to orange to red to blue.

Reginald's back, Nikki's face, and Maurice's arms had healed more or less instantly once they'd tumbled into the basement. The door had had a lock on it, but Nikki had stooped and snapped it easily. Once they were inside, there was little point in trying to secure the entrance, but Reginald ran a shovel through the inside handles just the same.

Now that night had come, they were free to leave the basement, but there were two problems: one, they didn't have anywhere to go, and two, the vampires at the Asbury were free to move around as well. Reginald was still mentally exhausted, and had slept most of the day. He didn't want to try another daring escape but felt sure he could if needed, especially if they had more room to maneuver — a luxury they hadn't had inside of the Council.

Maurice and Nikki had already marveled at their escape. Maurice said he'd never fought so well, and Nikki said the same. "It was like I couldn't miss," said Maurice. "I just swung and moved and dove, and somehow did it perfectly every time."

When Reginald explained his perception of events, the others looked at him as if he had barfed up a Buick. They said they had no experience of being led or of communicating with Reginald. But that made sense, Reginald decided. Their minds couldn't possibly process signals as quickly, on a conscious level, as he was sending them. Instead, they'd received Reginald's directions as subconscious suggestions.

"That means you can control vampire minds," Maurice told him.

"Only the minds of vampires I'm related to by blood," said Reginald.

"Quick," said Nikki. "Make me take off my top." Despite their peril, Nikki had been fighting her usual cravings for food and sex all day. She'd always had more experience fighting the former.

"Yes, do that," Maurice said to Reginald.

Once it was dark outside, Maurice wanted to move. He thought it was too risky to be so close to such a large collection of those who wanted them dead, but Reginald saw it as a brilliant hiding place for the same reason — hiding in plain sight. Eventually, they decided to move when Nikki cast the deciding vote on Maurice's side, but nobody knew where to go. They couldn't go to Maurice's house, or Reginald's house, or Nikki's apartment. They certainly couldn't go to the office.

Reginald found himself thinking of Todd Walker. He was truly an orphan now, and if the vampires at the Council didn't kill him, he'd be raised by killers. Remembering how Walker was earlier, the notion was nothing but terrible.

They'd spent much of the day using their cell phones to call people who needed to know their predicament. The list was very small. Maurice called his wife and a few friends. Reginald called his mother and Nikki called her sister. All three of them, throughout the day, tried to call Claire's house and the hospital where her mother was still convalescing, but they got nowhere. Victoria was asleep, and twice the person they spoke to said that there was no little girl around to hand the phone to. The one time a nurse reported that there *was* a girl in the room, said girl told the nurse that she didn't want to talk.

"She blames me," said Reginald.

"She blames all of us," said Nikki.

But it bothered all three of them, because both Claire and Victoria made obvious targets for the Council's ire. All they could do was to hope that the Nation was too distracted as it disintegrated to think of revenge or tidying up loose ends. They certainly hadn't tidied up the Council, which, by the way, would make a nice, stationary target should attack be in Reginald's plans.

For the moment, attack very much wasn't in any of their plans.

It was over. The Council was falling apart, the entire Nation was out of control, and the vampires of at least the United States were free to kill, and kill, and kill until they'd righted the balance enough to please the imagined whim of their creators.

"At least we can watch the action unfold on Fangbook," said Nikki. She'd been trying to get at the network all day from her phone, but there was no data coverage in the basement.

"And vote," said Maurice. "I, personally, am planning to vote against everything Charles mentions, just to be a dick."

"About that," said Reginald. "You said that you were worried that they wouldn't have a leader. But they will have a leader, and it won't be good."

"I'd figured that out," said Maurice.

"It'll be Charles," said Reginald.

"I've changed my mind. I'm going to go back and tell them that it's cool to just wander aimlessly, without direction."

"Get me my Coke back," said Reginald. He'd left an open can in the Council room and had been complaining all day about being thirsty. Nikki offered him her blood, saying it would at least satisfy the feeling in his mouth. Reginald made disgusted sounds.

They were all sitting on the floor, in a triangle, all of their legs pointing at roughly the same spot in the middle of the floor. They'd decided to get up and move to a different hiding spot, but nobody knew where that might be. Inertia was currently winning a hard-fought battle with sensibility. It had been an exhausting night.

"We need to go," said Maurice.

"Where?" said Nikki.

"Somewhere I can get a Coke," said Reginald.

Nobody got up.

"I don't know where to hide," said Reginald. "I don't know what to do about all this killing. I don't know what to do about the Vampire Nation, the Council, or Charles Barkley."

"Maybe Charles Barkley will get assassinated by those he serves," said Maurice.

"I was talking about the basketball player," said Reginald.

"So was I," said Maurice.

Reginald kicked a rock. It skittered across the floor and into a corner. He really did want a Coke.

"I don't know what to do about *Claire*," said Nikki. Nikki had become very possessive of Claire since becoming a vampire. She'd never have children in the literal sense, and Reginald suspected that Claire was her way of reconciling the conflict she seemed to feel about it.

Reginald stood up. "I want a Coke," he said. "So I'm overcoming my sloth, and am ready to go."

Maurice stood up, nodded, and said, "I want a crepe."

Nikki reluctantly dragged herself off of the floor, then brushed at her clothing to free it of dust. She looked at Maurice. "You don't like human food," she said.

"No, but I like the *idea* of crepes. I like a culture that *makes* crepes. And on a totally unrelated topic, I thought of a good place for us to hide."

Reginald took a deep breath, clearing his mind should he require his concentration during their exit. They wouldn't be able to take the car. One of the others would have to carry him, and they'd have to run all the way to the airport.

"Take the back roads, driver," said Reginald after he'd hopped up onto Maurice's back in the alley, like an oversized piggyback rider. Nikki looked over at the pair and laughed out loud. After the night and day they'd had, it was good to hear her laugh.

"But head for the terminal, not your buddy's cargo hanger," Reginald added. "I want a Coke."

The three vampires vanished in two blurring lines, exhausted but with at least a destination in mind, content to forget the world for at least a little while.

To Be Continued...

Reginald's story continues in *Fat Vampire 4: Harder Better Fatter Stronger*. Look for it on Amazon.com or wherever you bought this book!

Get Cool Stuff!

If you liked *Fat Vampire*, you'll LOVE the other titles being put out by Realm & Sands. Go to RealmAndSands.com to check out all of our most popular titles.

To be the first to know about all Realm & Sands releases (and to get our exclusive, free, email-only serials!), go to realmandsands.com.

More By Johnny B. Truant

For a full list of Johnny's books, visit:
johnnybtruant.com/books

Fat Vampire (books 1-6)
Unicorn Western (books 1-9)
Unicorn Genesis
The Beam
Namaste
Chupacabra Outlaw
The Bialy Pimps
Robot Proletariat
Space Shuttle
Greens
Everyone Gets Divorced

About Johnny B. Truant

Johnny B. Truant is an author, blogger, and podcaster who, like the Ramones, was long denied induction into the Rock and Roll Hall of Fame despite having a large cult following. He makes his online home at JohnnyBTruant.com and is the author of the *Fat Vampire* series and *The Bialy Pimps*, as well as co-authoring the political sci-fi thriller *The Beam* and the *Unicorn Western* series with Sean Platt... plus zillions of other things that we can't keep up with here.

Johnny, Sean Platt, and David Wright host two podcasts -- the Self Publishing Podcast and Better Off Undead -- both of which are available in the usual podcast places.

Johnny is also the kind of person who writes his bio in the third person.

You can connect with Johnny/me on Twitter as @JohnnyBTruant and you should totally send Johnny/me an email at johnny@johnnybtruant.com if the mood strikes you.

Also, if you liked the book you just read, I would REALLY, REALLY, REALLY appreciate if you'd leave me a review. Reviews make all the difference for independent authors.

Thanks for supporting my work!

Made in the USA
Coppell, TX
29 June 2020